Pictures from . . . Pilgrim's Progress

C. H. Spurgeon

A Commentary on Portions of John Bunyan's Immortal Allegory

With Prefatory Note by

THOMAS SPURGEON

This title and other C. H. Spurgeon works, including the **NEW PARK STREET PULPIT, THE METROPOLITAN TABERNACLE PULPIT, THE TREASURY OF DAVID,** and **THE SWORD AND THE TROWEL** are published by - -

 Pilgrim PUBLICATIONS
P.O. Box 66, Pasadena, Texas 77501
1992
ISBN 1-56186-201-0

JOHN BUNYAN
(1628-1688)

EDITOR'S INTRODUCTION.

WHEN it was first reported to me that a series of addresses on "The Pilgrim's Progress" had been discovered, I rejoiced as one that findeth great spoil, for I hoped that after enriching the pages of "The Sword and the Trowel" these fragrant flowers might be gathered together into a delightful nosegay. In the mercy of God, my hopes have been fulfilled. Month by month, the "Pictures" have appeared, for nearly a year and a half, in the Magazine, and abundant testimony is to hand that they have proved welcome to its readers. And now the full time has come for the issue of the book, and here it is—a sparkling circlet now that the gems are strung together.

Three additional "Pictures" will be found herein, to-wit: "Christian at the Cross," "Christian and Apollyon," and "Vanity Fair." It is not a little surprising that no trace could be found of any reference in the course of lectures to these outstanding features of the story. It does not follow, however, that the great preacher passed them by. Possibly they were not reported, or the MSS. may have gone astray. A little search in C. H. Spurgeon's Sermons and other works secured sufficient, and, I venture to think, appropriate material for the missing sketches. So in love with John Bunyan, and so akin to him in faith and thought and language was the Pastor of the Metropolitan Tabernacle, that I am persuaded another volume could be compiled comprising "Pictures" of other striking scenes and characters in the glorious allegory. Who can doubt that abundant material could be found in "The Spurgeon Library" for "Pictures" of "Christian under Mount Sinai," "Hill Difficulty," "Doubting Castle," "Little Faith," "Beulah Land," and "Valiant for Truth," for instance?

There is internal evidence that these addresses were delivered at Monday-evening prayer-meetings with the special purpose of edifying such as had just begun to go on pilgrimage. "You young converts," said the preacher again and again, in his personal and incisive style. Nevertheless, the more advanced in his congregation, I am certain, were eager and delighted listeners, too. So will it be with this book. Here is milk for babes and meat for men. Moreover, the meat is such that the "babes" will enjoy a taste of it, and the "men" will be all the better for a sip or two of the milk.

C. H. Spurgeon was a past-master in the art of commenting. Who that ever heard him did not rejoice as much in his exposition of the Scriptures as in his prayers and sermons? He has commented in print on the Psalms (The Treasury of David), and on Matthew (The Gospel of the Kingdom), and on Manton (Illustrations and Mediations, or Flowers from a Puritan's Garden) ; and here we have his Commentary on The Pilgrim's Progress, "that sweetest of all prose poems" as he himself describes it.

It is easy to see that the Commentator is in sympathy with his Author, and that he loves his task. If Mr. Spurgeon were ever prevailed upon to fill up a page of the once-popular Confession Album, I am pretty sure that his answer to the query, "Who is your favorite author?" was, "John Bunyan." He has spoken of him over and over again as "my great favorite," and has left it on record that he had read The Pilgrim's Progress at least one hundred times. The reason for his liking is not far to seek. They both loved "The Book of Books." Urging the earnest study of the Scriptures, C. H. Spurgeon once said: "Oh, that you and I might get into the very heart of the Word of God, and get that Word into ourselves! As I have seen the silkworm eat into the leaf, and consume it, so ought we to do with the Word of the Lord—not crawl over its surface, but eat right into it till we have taken it into our inmost parts. It is

idle merely to let the eye glance over the words, or
to recollect the poetical expressions, or the historic
facts; but it is blessed to eat into the very soul of the
Bible until, at last, you come to talk in Scriptural
language, and your very style is fashioned upon Scripture models, and, what is better still, your spirit is
flavored with the words of the Lord. I would quote
John Bunyan as an instance of what I mean. Read
anything of his, and you will see that it is almost like
reading the Bible itself. He had read it till his very
soul was saturated with Scripture; and, though his
writings are charmingly full of poetry, yet he cannot
give us his *Pilgrim's Progress*—that sweetest of all
prose poems—without continually making us feel and
say, 'Why, this man is a living Bible!' Prick him
anywhere; his blood is Bibline, the very essence of
the Bible flows from him. He cannot speak without
quoting a text, for his very soul is full of the Word
of God. I commend his example to you, beloved."

Moreover, the language of The Illustrious Dreamer
was to the mind of the Tabernacle Pastor. They
spake the same tongue. In an address delivered in
1862 on the occasion of the restoration of Bunyan's
tomb, Mr. Spurgeon assured his hearers that Bunyan's
works would not try their constitutions as might those
of Gill and Owen. "They are pleasant reading," said

he, "for Bunyan wrote and spoke in simple Saxon, and was a diligent reader of the Bible in the old version."

It was doubtless my dear father's intention to publish these addresses, for he had commenced the revision of them. Would that he had been able to accomplish the task. They would have been much more perfect then. As it is, we have them very much as he uttered them. There is no mistaking his voice in these sententious sentences.

I fancy that if he had been spared to issue these homilies, and to write an introduction, he would have urged his readers, as he did his hearers on the occasion referred to above, to raise a monument to John Bunyan in their hearts, to become his descendants by imbibing the truth that he taught, and to keep his memory green by living in his faith.

May the perusal of these pages create a love for the book which they explain and apply, as well as for the Book with which both the writers were "saturated."

THOMAS SPURGEON.

Clapham, 1903.

CHRISTIAN AND HOPEFUL PASS OVER THE RIVER OF DEATH
"Christian brake out with a loud voice, 'Oh! I see Him again.'"

CONTENTS.

CHRISTIAN

"I saw a man clothed in rags, a book in his hand, and a great burden on his back."

I.
PLIABLE SETS OUT WITH CHRISTIAN.

NEXT to the Bible, the book that I value most is John Bunyan's "Pilgrim's Progress." I believe I have read it through at least a hundred times. It is a volume of which I never seem to tire; and the secret of its freshness is that it is so largely compiled from the Scriptures. It is really Biblical teaching put into the form of a simple yet very striking allegory.

It has been upon my mind to give a series of addresses upon "The Pilgrim's Progress," for the characters described by John Bunyan have their living representatives to-day, and his words have a message for many who are found in our congregations at the present time.

You remember that, when Christian, with "a book in his hand, and a great burden upon his back," cried out, "What shall I do to be saved?" he "saw a man named Evangelist coming to him," who pointed him to the wicket-gate and the shining light. Then Bunyan says:

"So I saw, in my dream, that the man began to run. Now, he had not run far from his own door, but his wife and chil-

dren perceiving it, began to cry after him to reurn; but the
man put his fingers in his ears, and ran on, crying, 'Life! life!
eternal life!' (Luke xiv. 26.)   So he looked not behind him,
but fled towards the middle of the plain (Gen. xix. 17).

"The neighbours also came out to see him run (Jer. xx. 10) ;
and as he ran, some mocked, others threatened, and some
cried after him to return.   Now, among those that did so,
there were two that were resolved to fetch him back by force;
the name of the one was Obstinate, and the name of the other
Pliable."

Instead of yielding to them, Christian began at once
to plead with them to go along with him.   Obstinate
met all his pleas with mockery and abuse, but Pliable
was easily persuaded to go.   He is a type of those
who, apparently, set out for Heaven; but who have
not the root of the matter in them, and, therefore, soon
turn back.   The likeness that Bunyan has drawn of
him is worthy of our attentive consideration, for it is
true in every line.

It is significant that, in the first instance, Pliable
went with Obstinate upon the evil errand of endeavour-
ing to bring Christian back to the City of Destruction.
In like manner, some of those who have been in the
habit of keeping the worst of company may, sometimes, even without the operation upon them of the
grace of God, be induced to forsake their evil companions, and to cast in their lot, for a season, with
the followers of Christ.

These Pliable people, who are still a very numerous family, are very dependent upon those by whom they are surrounded. If they happen to have been born in a godly household, it is probable that they will make a profession of religion. It is even possible that they will be highly esteemed, and perhaps for years will bear a most reputable Christian character. If, on the other hand, they happen to be thrown among bad companions, they will be very easily allured by them, and be made to drink, to swear, and to fall into all the vices of the stronger persons by whom they are influenced. They scarcely seem to be men. They are mere jelly fish, swept along by every turn of the tide. They lack the true element of manhood, which is firmness. This, by the way, Obstinate had in excess. If you could put an Obstinate and a Pliable together, and make them one, you might, speaking of the natural man, have something more nearly approaching true manliness than either of them would be separately. Obstinate had all the firmness, while Pliable had none of it.

I think Pliable was a mouldable sort of creature; and, hence, Obstinate did with him as he liked until the poor feeble fellow came into the grasp of a stronger man than Obstinate, namely, Christian. After all, there is no man who is a match for a Christian in the matter of influence. There is a force about the truth, which is committed to our charge, when it is brought into fair play, that is not equalled by any form of lies. If a man's mind is really pliable, there is no doubt that an earnest Christian, who has been led by Divine grace to walk in the right road, will have wonderful control over such a person. So strong was Christian's influence that, even while Obstinate was reviling, Pliable rebuked him, and said: "My heart inclines to go with my neighbour." Christian had not said very much; he had not appeared to exercise much influence; but something had already told on Pliable. In the very presence and look of a Christian, there is a power over the heart of man. Moreover, influence grows; so it came to pass that Pliable presently went even further, and boldly declared: "I intend to go along with this good man, and to cast in my lot with him."

You perceive, however, that Pliable had no burden on his back, as Christian had. This was one of the proofs that he was not a true pilgrim. That which brings men to Christ is a sense of their need of Him. Albeit the sense of sin is not a qualification for salvation, yet it is the only motive that ever leads men to trust in Jesus; it is the impetus which Divine grace uses when it is drawing or driving men to the Saviour. Pliable did not, at first, appear to be greatly troubled when he heard that the City of Destruction was doomed; but when Christian talked so prettily about Heaven, he thought there might be something in it; indeed, he felt that there must be, when a man like Christian could leave his family and his business to go on a long pilgrimage; so he judged that, probably, he might do better himself if he went with Christian. But, all the while, there was no burden on his back; he had no sense of his need of a Saviour, and this was a very serious defect, to begin with, in one who was professing to go on pilgrimage to the Celestial City.

You will observe, too, that the only thing which tempted Pliable to go was Christian's talk about the "inheritance incorruptible, undefiled, and that fadeth not away." There are some preachers who can descant so prettily upon Heaven—the blessed associations of that happy country where they

"Meet to part no more,"—

that half their hearers are constrained to say, "We also will set out." These divines talk of the wall of jasper, the gates of pearl, the street of gold, the sea of glass, and the emerald rainbow round about the throne, in such a way that persons of a poetical temperament, and especially those of a pliable disposition, have their emotions excited by the descriptions which give only a material view of what was intended to be understood in a spiritual sense. They really think that Heaven is, literally, what the Book of the Revelation says it is figuratively. They never get at the kernel of the inward sense; it is the husk of the outward meaning that at. acts them. They are satisfied, charmed, bewitched, fascinated by that, so they resolve to set out on the journey.

To tell the whole truth about Mr. Pliable, I must say that he began exceedingly well. I have already reminded you that he defended Christian when Obstinate reviled him; and when Obstinate turned his abuse upon Pliable, and said, "What! more fools still?" he did not seem to wince under it. Some of these pliable people will even bear a great deal of persecution, and be content to be ridiculed, and laughed at; they will even suffer loss rather than turn back. If they do this really "for Christ's sake," it is well; but, often, it is only borne with a view to self-aggrandizement, and in order to obtain something better by way of recompense, so that it is selfishness still that rules them. They give up a little of the good that there is in this world—and it is not very much, after all, that they sacrifice—for the sake of the better world that is yet to be revealed. They will not give up all that they have—"house, or brethren, or sisters, or father, or mother, or wife, or children, or lands"—for Christ's sake, and the Gospel's, and therefore they are not Christ's true disciples. They are prepared to make some small sacrifice, but only for the sake of winning Heaven or of escaping hell.

Observe the way in which Christian treated Pliable after Obstinate left them. I daresay he had known him before and understood quite well what a soft, easy-going fellow he was, and how very readily he might be twisted either one way or another; yet he did not disdain his company, but said to him: "Come, neighbour Pliable, I am glad you are persuaded to go along with me." You and I, dear friends, are bound to invite men to come to Christ no matter who or what they may be; and we should try to encourage them all we can, even though we may have in our own heart a well-grounded fear that some of them will not hold out to the end. I do not think it is for us to say to young persons, who seem to be in earnest about spiritual matters, that we are afraid they will not persevere, and so discourage them. Our business is rather to say to each one of them: "Come, neighbour, come with me, and you shall fare as I do." It is the work of the Spirit to fill the Gospel net; it is our duty to throw it, and drag it along the bottom; and whether we catch good fish or bad, is not so much our concern

as our Master's. Christian, though not yet at peace
himself, had a commendable love for others. It is a
beautiful trait, which I like to see in those who feel
the secondary work of grace in their souls, that they
want others to feel as they feel. This conduct on the
part of Christian ought to be a lesson to some of you
who have long had joy and peace in believing, but
who do not say to others: "Come, neighbour Pliable."
Seek to have in yourselves something of the zeal and
compassion of this poor pilgrim with a troubled conscience, yet with a sympathetic heart.

So Pliable, without counting the cost, or reckoning
for a moment upon all the difficulties of the way, set
out, in a thoughtless, light-hearted manner, upon that
journey which will always prove too long for those
who start on it in their own strength alone. As they
went over the plain, Christian began to talk to Pliable
of what he himself had felt—"the powers and terrors
of what is unseen";—but, directly he did so, Pliable
changed the subject. He did not want to know anything about such matters; he had, in fact, taken the
whole thing in a carnal sense; and, as for the powers
and terrors of the unseen world, he knew nothing at
all about them; and, apparently, he did not want to
know about them, for he harked back to that which
had attracted him at the first, and said to Christian:

"Tell me now further, what the things are, and how to be enjoyed, whither we are going."

These two men, as they went along walking and talking, fell into the error of speaking a good deal about things which neither of them properly understood. It is true that Christian said: "Since you are desirous to know, I will read of them in my Book." There was that good element in their conversation, which we can cordially commend; still, even that may not be the wisest thing for young beginners to do. It is, indeed, a wise thing to read the Bible, and to talk of what it contains; but this must be done with much prayer if it is to be of real spiritual benefit. I look in vain for any word about Pliable praying, but I do read concerning Christian, even before he started on his pilgrimage—

"He would also walk solitarily in the fields, sometimes reading, sometimes praying; and thus for some days he spent his time. Now, I saw upon a time when he was walking in the fields, that he was, as he was wont, reading in his Book, and greatly distressed in his mind; and as he read, he burst out as he had done before, crying, 'What shall I do to be saved?' (Acts xvi. 30, 31.)"

It was not so with Pliable. What he heard Christian read from the Book did not make him sorrowful, but enchanted and delighted him. He only thought of the Celestial Country, not of the plague of his own

heart, nor of the damnable nature of his sin. These
things had never come home with power to him as
they had to Christian, and therefore he did not say:
"Come, let us kneel together, and plead for mercy;"
but he said, "Well, my good companion, glad am
I to hear of these things; come on, let us mend our
pace." Yes, at first, there are none who are so enthusiastic as these empty, hollow ones. "Let us mend
our pace," said Pliable. Surely, brethren, the advice
is good, but I do not like it from such lips. It is a very
proper exhortation in its place, but not when it comes
from one who has never been burdened on account of
sin, nor broken under the hammer of God's law, nor
made to feel his own nothingness and worthlessness.
You who are empty may well travel quickly; you who
never felt the load of sin upon your hearts may well
run swiftly. Pliable is all for pushing on, making
a stir, and creating a noise. He attends revival services, and likes to have them protracted; when the
fit is on him, he would be willing to be up all night,
to turn his house out of the windows, and to do all
manner of extraordinary things, all to show how full
of zeal he is. But, in a little time, it will be all over.
It is like the crackling of thorns under a pot, which
burn so fiercely that they make the pot boil over, and
put the fire out.

"Come," said Pliable, "let us mend our pace." Christian said, "I cannot go so fast as I would, by reason of this burden that is on my back." Then, just as they ended their talk, Bunyan tells us that "they drew near to a very miry slough that was in the midst of the plain; and they, being heedless, did both fall suddenly into the bog. The name of the slough was Despond."

PLIABLE   OBSTINATE

CHRISTIAN AND PLIABLE IN THE SLOUGH OF DESPOND

"Christian still endeavored to struggle toward the side of the
slough which was farthest from his own house."

II.

THE TWO PILGRIMS IN THE SLOUGH.

THROUGH their much talking, and little praying, and giving no heed to where they were going, Christian and Pliable all of a sudden found themselves floundering in the Slough of Despond. Bunyan says:

"Here, therefore, they wallowed for a time, being grievously bedaubed with the dirt; and Christian, because of the burden that was on his back, began to sink in the mire."

Even then, had they but known where to look, they might have discovered that there were, "by the direction of the Lawgiver, certain good and substantial steps, placed even through the very midst of this Slough." Had they set their feet upon these steps—in other words, had the pilgrims trusted the promises of God—they might have gone through to the other side with scarcely a stain upon their garments.

I always feel inclined to blame Evangelist for some of the discomfort that poor Christian suffered in the Slough of Despond. I am a great lover of John Bunyan, but I do not believe him infallible; and the other day I met with a story about him which I think a very good one. There was a young man, in Edinburgh, who wished to be a missionary. He was a wise young man; so he thought, "If I am to be a missionary, there is no need for me to transport myself far away from home; I may as well be a missionary in Edinburgh." There's a hint to some of you ladies, who give away tracts in your district, and never give your servant Mary one. Well, this young man started, and determined to speak to the first person he met. He met one of those old fishwives; those of us who have seen them can never forget them, they are extraordinary women indeed. So. stepping up to her, he said, "Here you are, coming along with your burden on your back; let me ask you if you have got another burden, a spiritual burden." "What!" she asked; "do you mean that burden in John Bunyan's *Pilgrim's Progress?* Because, if you do, young man, I got rid of that many years ago, probably before you were born. But I went a better way to work than the pilgrim did. The Evangelist that John Bunyan talks about was one of your parsons that do not preach the Gospel; for he said, 'Keep that light in thine eye, and run to the wicket-gate.' Why, man alive! that was not the place for him to run to. He should have said, 'Do you see that cross? Run there at once!'

But instead of that, he sent the poor pilgrim to the wicket-gate first; and much good he got by going there!" "But did you not," the young man asked, "go through any Slough of Despond?" "Yes, I did; but I found it a great deal easier going through with my burden off than with it on my back."

The old woman was quite right. John Bunyan put the getting rid of the burden too far from the commencement of the pilgrimage. If he meant to show what usually happens, he was right; but if he meant to show what ought to have happened, he was wrong. We must not say to the sinner: "Now, sinner, if thou wilt be saved, go to the baptismal pool; go to the wicket-gate; go to the church; do this or that." No, the cross should be right in front of the wicket-gate; and we should say to the sinner: "Throw thyself down there, and thou art safe; but thou art not safe till thou canst cast off thy burden, and lie at the foot of the cross, and find peace in Jesus."

Now let us leave Christian for a little while, and turn our thoughts to his companion, Pliable. This experience in the Slough of Despond was the first trial he had met with since he had started on pilgrimage. It was, comparatively, a slight one. The Slough was not likely to swallow them up. It was not nearly so bad as lying in Giant Despair's dungeon, or fighting with Apollyon in the Valley of Humiliation. It was not much for anyone to endure, but it was more than Pliable could stand. Bunyan thus describes what happened to him:

"At this, Pliable began to be offended, and angrily said to his fellow, 'Is this the happiness you have told me all this while of? If we have such ill speed at our first setting out, what may we expect betwixt this and our journey's end? May I get out again with my life, you shall possess the brave country alone for me.' And with that he gave a desperate struggle or two, and got out of the mire on that side of the Slough which was next to his own house. So away he went, and Christian saw him no more."

In like fashion, it often comes to pass that, without any great outward trial, but simply through despondency of mind, a sudden damper pales the flush of early joy, and some of those who set out on the road to Heaven turn back, and so prove that they did not start aright, and never had the work of God, the Holy Ghost, truly in their souls.

Some of you, dear friends, when you are attending the services here, or meeting with your companions in one or other of our many Bible-classes, get very warm, and excited, and enthusiastic; and then, perhaps, you have to go away to live in the country, which is like going out of a hothouse into an icewell, and straightway you forget all about the happy experi-

ences that you enjoyed amongst us. Or it may be
that, instead of your hearing a comforting and sooth-
ing sermon, some Sunday morning, I preach an
arousing, heart-searching one, and you are offended,
or frightened, and give up all desire to tread the pilgrim pathway.

> "The fearful soul that tires and faints,
>   And walks the ways of God no more,
> Is but esteem'd almost a saint,
>   And makes his own destruction sure."

Beware, I pray you, of any religion that merely
springs from the carnal desire of enjoyment of Heaven.
Both the terrors of hell and the joys of Heaven are
insufficient to make the soul seek the Saviour truly.
There must be a sense of sin and a desire after holiness,
because, after all, the essence of hell is sin, and the
essence of Heaven is holiness, and you are not likely
to go to God merely because of the external hell or
Heaven. You will only be led to trust in Jesus Christ
through the essence of the two external things, namely,
sin pressing upon you, and your soul crying out after
purity, and holiness, and likeness to God.

May God grant that we may not have any Pliables
in our church! Alas! we do get them sometimes, and
they go a great deal further on the pilgrim's road than
Mr. Bunyan describes. They go right by the Inter-

preter's House; they climb up the Hill Difficulty;
they even pass the cross; but, of course, they never
feel their burden roll off their backs. They are not
conscious that there is a burden there. When Christians sing, they also sing because they think they are
to have the same inheritance by-and-by. They generally go through the Valley of Humiliation in broad
daylight. Apollyon never fights with them, and they
wonder how it is that he does not assail them. They
think what good people they are, and what bad
people they must be who have those stirrings and
smitings of conscience of which they hear us speak.
They cannot understand why we talk about Christians
having such fierce conflicts within; but if they really
knew the Lord, they would soon understand all about
it; and until they do know Him, much of our preaching must remain a mystery to them. Pliable was an
utter stranger to vital godliness. He had converted
himself; or, rather, Christian had converted him by
his talk about Heaven; and, perhaps, if it had not
been for the Slough of Despond, he would have gone,
as Ignorance did, right to the river side, and been
ferried over by Vain-hope, only to be refused admis-
sion at the gate, and to be carried by the two Shining
Ones, bound hand and foot, and to be cast into hell
by the back door, for there is a back door to hell as

well as a front one; and some professors, who have, apparently, gone very far on the road to Heaven, will ultimately go to hell by this door unless they repent of their sin, and believe in our Lord Jesus Christ.

But what became of Pliable after he struggled out of the Slough of Despond? Bunyan says:

"Now, I saw in my dream, that by this time Pliable was got home to his house again; so that his neighbours came to visit him, and some of them called him wise man for coming back; and some called him fool for hazarding himself with Christian; others again did mock at his cowardliness; saying, 'Surely, since you began to venture, I would not have been so base as to have given out for a few difficulties.' So Pliable sat sneaking among them."

There is one thing about the world that I have often admired. We sometimes say, "Give the devil his due," and I will give the world its due. I mean that, when a man goes a little way in religion, and then turns back, mere worldlings generally despise him. I believe that the wicked world has a genuine respect for a true Christian. It hates him, and that is the only homage it is able to pay him. The reason why the men of our Saviour's day hated and mocked Him, was because they had what I may call an awful respect for Him, and did not know how otherwise to express it. They hated and loathed what they could not rightly appreciate; and thus they showed, by their mockery and scorn, how far they were from comprehending the excellence of the Saviour. You must expect similar treatment from the ungodly if you are like your Lord.

But when a pretended pilgrim turns back, they despise him; they call him a "turn-coat," and they could not very well hit upon a more correct name for him. "Oh!" say they, "a little while ago, you were with the earnest people, and you were, apparently, as earnest as they were; but what are you now?" Then, when the man is seen walking into the alehouse, you know how they greet him. "Ah, Mr. Sobersides! so you've come back, have you?" When they track him to the theatre, they say to him, "How long is it since you were at the Tabernacle?" or make some coarse joke about him. They know how to handle the whip of scorn, and I thank them for using it, and hope they will always lay on their blows right heavily.

But, mark you, the little scorn which Pliable finds it so hard to bear in this life is but a very slight foretaste of what he will have to bear in hell. You remember that remarkable description which is given by the prophet Isaiah of the king of Babylon, when he went down to hell, and all the kings whom he had destroyed, and whose countries he had ravaged, were lying on their beds of fire; and as they saw their great conqueror enter, instead of trembling, they hissed out, "Art *thou* also become weak as we? art thou become like unto us? How art thou fallen from heaven, O Lucifer, son of the morning! how art thou cut down to the ground, which didst weaken the nations!"

If any of you turn back, as Pliable did, this will be the worst element in your everlasting torment, that you did, after a fashion, set out on the road to Heaven, that you did pretend to be a Christian, that you said you had enlisted under the banner of the cross, that you talked a good deal about your experience, that you went to the prayer-meeting, and perhaps even prayed audibly, that you gave away tracts, and yet that you were, after all, only a hypocrite, and therefore found yourself, at the last, amid the flames of hell. If I must perish, let it be as a sinner who has never professed to be a saint, rather than as a Pliable, who started for the Celestial City, and then returned to his home in the City of Destruction. It would have been better for those, who have had the taste of heavenly things in their mouths, and yet have not "tasted that the Lord is gracious," if they had never known anything at all about the way of righteousness.

Some of you, dear friends, must be either Pliables or Christians; you have, naturally, such a disposition that you cannot help being easily influenced by your

associates; and unless the grace of God shall make
you a child of God, you will be led astray from Him.
You cannot be Obstinate; you are too good—as we
use the word "good" in a common way—you are
too kind, too affectionate, and altogether too tender-
hearted to act as that man did towards Christian.
You could not bring yourself down to drink or swear;
your mother's influence and your father's example
have too much power over you for you to become an
Obstinate. You cannot sin as others can; you cannot
sin in ignorance. I was almost going to say, I wish
you could. If you are to be lost, if you do not mean
to believe in our Lord Jesus Christ, if you are determined to perish, it were far better for you to perish as
Tyre and Sidon, than as Bethsaida, or Chorazin, or
Capernaum.

I believe that, when some of you get into this
Tabernacle, you feel that you must be Pliables. There
are a few, in this congregation, whom I happen to
know personally, who cannot help coming to hear me,
though they remain unsaved. I preach at them, and
they know I do, and respect me for it, and even thank
me for it, and sometimes say that they hope they
will be converted one day; but they are so pliable that
they will weep under a sermon, and, after a fashion,
pray; but when they get away from here, there is a

stronger hand than mine that lays hold of them.
Some companion says to them, "Come along; never
mind what Spurgeon says, come along with me;" and
they cannot say "No." They have not the moral
courage to say they will not go where the ungodly
lead them. Whenever they are tempted to sin, they
yield. They wish there were no tempters, and that
they could get into a world where goodness was in the
ascendant. They are like a sailing-vessel, which de-
pends on every wind, and is blown hither and thither
by every breeze. They have no inward force to enable
them to resist. This is not the way to get to Heaven.
You need, as it were, a Divine engine mightily at
work, with all its heaving, panting energy, that you
may make headway against winds and waves, and keep
straight on, at the same rate, always steadily advanc-
ing towards the far-off port.

May God, by His grace, bring you to this blessed
condition! I should have liked to have spoken to you
so effectively that you could not have forgotten what
I said, but would have gone home to think about it,
and to pray about it, and to believe it. I should like
you even to wish that you had never been born, because then I should hope that you would wish to be
born again. There is no hope for you else. You have
been born once; there is no possibility of your getting

over the fact that you have your being. Ask the Lord that you may have your being in Christ Jesus. You are a creature, and the only hope for you is to be made "a new creature in Christ Jesus." May the Holy Spirit bring you to this point! Ask Him to do so. The best place to get a sense of sin is at the foot of the cross. May my blessed Master meet you there, and draw you to Himself, and so may you be saved, and not be found amongst the Pliables at the last! Amen.

III.

THE MAN WHOSE NAME WAS HELP.

"Wherefore Christian was left to stumble in the Slough of Despond alone; but still he endeavoured to struggle to that side of the Slough that was still further from his own house, and next to the Wicket-gate; the which he did, but could not get out, because of the burden that was upon his back. But I beheld, in my dream, that a man came to him, whose name was Help, and asked him what he did there.

"CHR. 'Sir,' said Christian, 'I was bid go this way by a man called Evangelist, who directed me also to yonder gate, that I might escape the wrath to come; and as I was going thither, I fell in here.'

"HELP. 'But why did you not look for the steps?'

"CHR. 'Fear followed me so hard, that I fled the next way and fell in.'

"Then said he, 'Give me thy hand.' So he gave him his hand, and he drew him out, and set him upon sound ground, and bid him go on his way (Psalm xl. 2)."

ACCORDING to the diversity of gifts which proceeded from the self-same Spirit of God, those who laboured in guiding wayfarers to the Celestial City, in the early ages of Christianity, fulfilled different offices, and were known by different names. Paul tells us, in his first Letter to the Corinthian Pilgrims

(1 Cor. xii. 28), "God hath set some in the Church, first apostles." These were to go from place to place, founding churches, and ordaining ministers. There were, "secondarily, prophets"; some of whom uttered prophecies, while others were gifted in explaining them. Then came, "thirdly, teachers"; who were, probably, either pastors settled over divers churches, guiding pilgrims along the heavenward road, as Greatheart did, or men like Evangelist, journeying about to warn and direct such as they met.

"After that, miracles; then, gifts of healings;" and the apostle does not forget to mention another class of persons, called "HELPS." Who these people precisely were, it would be very difficult, at this period of time, if not quite impossible, to tell. Some, who are learned in the pilgrim records, have thought that they were assistant ministers, who occasionally aided settled pastors, both in the pastoral work of visiting, and also in preaching the Word. Others have supposed that they were assistant deacons, and perhaps even deaconesses, an office which was recognized in the apostolic churches. Others, again, have imagined these "helps" to have been the attendants in the sanctuary, who took care that strangers were properly accommodated, and managed those details, in connection with the gatherings of persons for united worship, which always must be superintended by somebody. Whoever they were, or whatever may have been their functions, they appear to have been a useful body of people, worthy to be mentioned in the same list as apostles, and prophets, and teachers, and even to be named with miracle-workers, and those who had the gifts of healing. It is very probable that they had no official standing, but were only moved by the natural impulse of the Divine life within them to do anything and everything which would assist either teacher, pastor, or deacon in the work of the Lord. They were of that class of brethren who are useful anywhere, who can always stop a gap, and who are only too glad when they find that they can make themselves serviceable to the Church of God in any capacity, however lowly. The Church in this age rejoices in a goodly brigade of "helps," but perhaps a word or two may stir up their pure minds by way of remembrance.

John Bunyan, whom we shall see to be the master of Christian experience as well as of holy allegory has, in the passage at the head of this chapter, described a part of the work of these "helps" which is most valuable, and most required. "The man whose name was Help" came to Christian when he was floundering in the foul morass of despondency. Just when the poor man was likely to have been choked, having missed his footing in the Slough, and when, with all his struggling, he was only sinking deeper and deeper into the mire, there suddenly came to him a person— of whom Bunyan says nothing more throughout his whole allegory, and here only tells us his name—who put out his hand, and speaking some words of encouragement to him, pulled him out of the mire, set him on the King's highway, and then went about his business—a man unknown to fame on earth, but enrolled in the annals of the skies as wise to win souls.

There are periods, in the Divine life, when the help of judicious Christian brethren is invaluable. Most of us, who are now rejoicing in a well-assured hope, have known quite as much as we wish to know about that awful Slough of Despond. I myself floundered in it for five years, or thereabouts, and am therefore well acquainted with its terrible geography. In some places, it is deeper than in others, and more nauseous; such as the spot where David was when he cried, "I sink in deep mire, where there is no standing"; but, believe me, a man may reckon himself thrice happy when he gets out of it; for, even at its best, when he is fairly in it, it threatens to swallow him up alive. Dear, very dear to us, must ever be the hand that helped us out of the horrible pit; and while we ascribe all the glory to the God of grace, we cannot but love most affectionately the instrument whom He sent to be the means of our deliverance.

On the summit of some of the Swiss passes, the Canton, for the preservation and accommodation of travellers, maintains a small body of men, who live in a little house on the mountain, and whose business it is to help travellers on their way. It was very pleasant, when we were toiling up the steep ascent of the Col D'Obbia, in Northern Italy, to see, some three or four miles from the top, a man coming down, who saluted us as though he had known us for years, and had been awaiting our arrival. He carried a spade in his hand; and though we did not know what was ahead of us, he evidently knew all about it, and was forearmed and prepared for every emergency. By-and-by, we came to deep snow, and our kind pioneer immediately went to work with his spade to clear a footway, along which he carried the weaker ones of the party upon his back. It was his business to care for travellers; and, ere long, he was joined by another, who brought with him refreshments for the weary ones. These men were "helps," who spent their lives on that part of the road where it was known that their services would frequently be in requisition. They would have been worth little in the plains; their attentions might even have been considered intrusive had they met us in any other place; but they were exceedingly valuable, because they presented themselves just where they were required, having, as it were, waylaid us with kindness.

"Helps" are of little use to a man when he can help himself; but when he is hopelessly slipping amid the slime of the Slough of Despond, then a man of affectionate heart becomes more precious than the gold of Ophir.

The men of this brigade of "helps," if I understand Bunyan aright, are stationed all round the borders of the great dismal Swamp of Despond; and it is their business to keep watch, and listen along the brink of the Slough for the cries of any poor benighted travellers who may be staggering in the mire. Just as the Royal Humane Society keeps its men along the borders of the lakes in the parks in wintertime, and when the ice is forming, bids them to be on the watch, and take care of any who may venture upon it, so, a little knot of Christian people, both men and women, should always be ready, in every church, to listen for cries of distress, and to watch for broken hearts and cast-down spirits. Such are the "helps" whom we need; and such, perhaps, were the ancient "helps" mentioned by Paul.

It may be well to give a few directions to these

"helps" as to how they may assist seeking sinners out of the Slough of Despond.

From my own pastoral experience, I am led to recommend a careful imitation of "the man whose name was Help" as he is described by Bunyan. So, first, when you meet with one who is despairing, *get him to state his own case.* When Help assisted Christian, he did not at once put out his hand to him; but he asked him what he did there, and why he did not look for the steps. It does men much good to make them unveil their spiritual griefs to their comforters. Confession to a priest is an abomination, but the communication of our spiritual difficulties to a fellow-Christian will often be a sweet relief and a helpful exercise. You, who seek to aid the awakened, will be wise, like the angels at the tomb, to enquire of the weeping Mary, "Woman, why weepest thou?" Their answers will direct the helper's line of action, and assist in the application of the necessary consolation. The patient who understands the malady will the more cheerfully yield to the treatment of a wise physician. I have occasionally found that the mere act of stating a difficulty has been the means of at once removing it. Some of the most distressing doubts, like hideous screech-owls, will not bear the light of day. There are many spiritual difficulties which, if a man did but look them fully and fairly in the face long enough to be able to describe them, would vanish during the investigation. "O thou of little faith, wherefore didst thou doubt?" is our Lord's way of setting reason in battle array against unbelief. Let the mourner state his case, by all means; and do you patiently listen to it. Get that young man alone, dear brother; ask him to sit down quietly with you, and then enquire of him, "What is the point that puzzles you? What cannot you understand? What is it that makes you so dejected and dispirited?" Wisely did good Help induce Christian to unbosom his griefs; do thou likewise.

Next to this, *enter, as much as lieth in you, into the case before you.* Help came to the brink of the Slough, and stooped down to his poor friend. This may seem to you, perhaps, as unimportant direction; but, depend upon it, you will be able to give very little help, if any, if you do not follow it. Sympathy is the mainspring of our ability to comfort others. If you cannot enter into a soul's distress, you will be no "Son of Consolation" to that soul. So, seek to bring yourselves down to "weep with them that weep," that you may uplift them to the platform of your joy. Do not sneer at a difficulty because it seems small to you; recollect that it may be very great to the person who is troubled by it. Do not begin to scold, and tell the anxious enquirer that he ought not to feel as he does feel, or to be distressed as he is. As God puts His everlasting arms underneath us, when we are weak, so you must put the outstretched arms of your sympathy underneath your younger and weaker brethren, that you may lift them up. If you see a brother in the mire, put your arms right down into the mud that, by the grace of God, you may lift him bodily out of it. Recollect that you were once just where that desponding sister of yours is now; and try, if you can, to bring back your own feelings when you were in her condition. It may be, as you say, that the stripling or damsel is very foolish. Yes, but you were yourself foolish once; and, then, you abhorred all manner of meat, and your soul drew near to the gates of death. You must, to use Paul's language, "become a fool for their sakes." You must put yourselves into the condition of these simple-minded ones. If you cannot do this, you need training to teach you how to be a help; as yet, you do not know the way.

Your next step may be, to *comfort these poor brethren with the promises of God.* Help asked Christian why he did not look for the steps; for there were good and substantial stepping-stones placed through the very midst of the Slough; but Christian said he had missed

them through excessive fear. We should point sinking
souls to the many precious promises of God's Word.
Brethren, mind that you are yourselves well acquainted
with the consoling declarations of Scripture; have
them on the tip of your tongue, ready for use at any
time that they are required. I have heard of a certain
scholar, who used to carry miniature copies of the
classic authors about with him, so that he seemed to
have almost a Bodleian Library in his pocket. Oh,
that you would carry miniature Bibles about with you;
or, better still, that you had the whole Word of God
hidden in your hearts, so that, like your Lord, you
"should know how to speak a word in season to him
that is weary"! "A word spoken in due season, how
good is it!" Whenever you come across a distressed
soul, what a blessed thing it is for you to be able to
say to him: "Yes, you are a sinner, it is true; but
Jesus Christ came into the world to save sinners!"
Possibly, he will tell you that he cannot do anything;
but you may answer that he is not told to do anything,
for it is written, "Believe on the Lord Jesus Christ,
and thou shalt be saved." He will, perhaps, reply that
he cannot believe; but you can remind him of the
promise, "Whosoever shall call upon the Name of the
Lord shall be saved."

Some texts in the Bible are like those constellations

in the heavens which are so conspicuous that, when the mariner once sees them, he knows in what direction he is steering. Certain brilliant passages of Scripture appear to be set in the firmament of Revelation as guiding stars to bewildered souls. Point to these. Quote them often. Rivet the sinner's eyes upon them. Thus shall you aid him most efficiently.

If a despairing soul should read these pages, let me quote to him these exceeding great and precious promises of our gracious God: "Let the wicked forsake his way, and the unrighteous man his thoughts: and let him return unto the Lord, and He will have mercy upon him; and to our God, for He will abundantly pardon." "He retaineth not His anger forever, because He delighteth in mercy." "Whosoever will, let him take the water of life freely." These three texts are specimens of the "steps" which "the Lord of the way" has caused to be placed where they can best assist sinking sinners.

After quoting the promises, *try to instruct those who may need your help more fully in the plan of salvation.* The Gospel is preached, every Sabbath day, in thousands of pulpits, yet there is nothing that is so little known or rightly understood as the truth as it is in Jesus. The preacher cannot, even with all his attempts, make the simple Gospel plain to some of his hearers; but you, who are no preachers, may be able to do it, because your state of mind and education may happen just to suit the comprehension of the person concerned. God is my witness how earnestly I always endeavor to make clear and plain whatever I say, but yet my peculiar modes of thought and expression may not be suitable to the cases of certain persons in my audiences. You, by holy tact and perseverance, may be able to cheer those hearts which gather not a gleam of light from me. If my brethren and sisters, the "helps," will be constantly and intelligently active, they may, by homely language, often explain where theologians only confuse; that which may not have been understood, in the form of scholastic divinity, may reach the heart when uttered in the language of daily life. We need parlour and kitchen and workshop preachers, who can talk the natural speech of men; Universities and Colleges often obscure the truth by their modes of speech. If you, our friends who mingle with the world, will only put the same thing in another shape, the sinner will say, "Ah! I see it now; I could not comprehend it from the pastor's language, but I can understand it from your plain talk." Do, if you would help souls, point them to the Saviour. Do not trouble them with irrelevant matters, but direct them at once to "the precious blood of Jesus," for that is the one source of pardon and cleansing. Tell the sinner that whosoever trusts in Jesus shall be saved. Do not point to the Wicket-gate, as Evangelist did; for that is not the truest way, but bid the sinner go straightway to the Cross. Poor Christian need not have wallowed in the Slough of Despond if he had met with a fully-instructed believer to direct him at the first. Do not scold the mistaken Evangelist, but seek, by always pointing the sinner to Calvary, to undo the mischief he wrought to the pilgrim.

Would you supplement this? Then, *tell the troubled one your own experience.* Many have been aided to escape from the Slough of Despond in this way. "What!" exclaims the young friend to whom we are speaking, "did *you* ever feel as I do?" I have often been amused, when I have been talking with enquirers, to see them open their eyes with amazement to think that I had ever felt as they did, whereas I should have opened mine with far greater astonishment if I had not. We tell our patients all their symptoms, and then they think we must have read their hearts; whilst the fact is, that our hearts are just like theirs, and, in reading ourselves, we read them. We have gone along the same road as they have, and it would be a very hard thing if we could not describe what we have ourselves undergone. Even advanced Christians often de-

rive great comfort from reading and hearing the experience of others, if it is anything like their own; and
to young people, it is a most blessed means of grace to
hear others tell what they have gone through before
them. I wish our elder brethren would be more frequently "helps" in this matter; and that, when they
see others in trouble, they would tell them that they
have passed through the very same difficulties, instead,
as some do, of blaming the young people for not knowing what they cannot know, and upbraiding them because they have not "old heads on young shoulders,"
where, by the way, they would be singularly out of
place.

Once more, you will very much help the young
enquirer *by praying with him*. Oh, the power of
prayer! When you cannot tell the sinner what you
want to say, you can sometimes tell it to God in the
sinner's hearing. There is a way of saying, in prayer
with a person, what you cannot say direct to his face;
and it is well, sometimes, when praying with another,
to put the case very plainly and earnestly—something
in this way, "Lord, Thou knowest that this poor
woman, now kneeling before Thee, is very much
troubled; but it is her own fault. She will not believe
in Thy love, because she says she feels no evidence of
it, Thou hast given evidence enough in the gift of

Thy dear Son; but she will persist in wanting to see something of her own upon which she may rest, some good frames or feelings. She has been told, many times, that all her hope lies in Christ, and not at all in herself; yet she will continue to seek fire in the midst of water, and life in the graves of death. Open her eyes, Lord; turn her face in the right direction, and lead her to look to Christ, and not to self!"

Praying in this way puts the case very plainly, and may be in itself useful. Moreover, there is a real power in prayer; the Lord assuredly hears the cry of His people still. As certainly as the electric fluid bears the message from one place to another, as certainly as the laws of gravitation control the spheres, so certainly is prayer a mysterious but a very real power. God does answer prayer. We are as sure of this as we are that we breathe: we have tried it, and proved it. It is not occasionally that God has heard us, but it has become as regular a thing with us to ask and have as it is for our children to ask us for food, and to receive it at our hands. I should hardly think of attempting to prove that God hears my prayer; I have no more doubt about it than I have of the fact that the law of gravitation affects me in walking, in sitting still, in rising up, and in lying down. Exercise, then, this power of prayer; and you shall often find that, when nothing else will help a soul out of its difficulty, supplication will do it. There are no limits, dear friends, if God be with you, to your ability to help others through the power of prayer.

These directions—and they are not very many— you should keep in your memories, as you would the directions of the Royal Humane Society, with reference to people who have been in danger of drowning.

IV.

"HELPS."

HAVING spoken about the best way of helping souls out of despondency and distress, I shall now proceed to describe those who may truly be called HELPS—for it is not everybody, and not even every professing Christian, who is qualified to perform this most needful work.

The first essential for a true "help" is, that *he should have a tender heart.* Some brethren are, by Divine grace, specially prepared and fitted to become soul-winners. I know an earnest brother, whom I have often called my hunting dog, for he is always on the watch for those who have been wounded by the Word. No sooner does he see that there are souls that appear to be anxious than he is on the alert; and whenever he hears of a meeting of converts, he is all astir. He may have appeared dull and heavy before, but, at such times, his eyes flash, his heart beats more quickly, his whole soul is moved to action, and he becomes like a new man. In other company, he might not feel at home; but, among converts and enquirers, he is all alive and happy. Where they are to be found, his heart takes fire directly; for, amidst the diversities of gifts that proceed from the one Spirit, his gift evidently is that of helping souls out of spiritual trouble. Such a man was Timothy, of whom Paul wrote to the Philippians, "I have no man like-minded, who will naturally care for your state."

You know that, in ordinary life, some people are born nurses, while others cannot nurse at all. If you were ill, you would not care to have them near you, even if they would come for nothing, or pay you for having them. Probably, they mean well; but, some-how or other, they have not the gentleness and tender-ness which are essential in a good nurse. They stamp across the room so heavily that they wake up their poor patient; and if there be any medicine to be taken at night, it tastes all the worse if they administer it to you. But, on the other hand, you have known a real nurse—perhaps your own wife—you never heard her walk across the room when you were ill, for she steps so softly that you might almost as soon hear her heart beat as hear her footfall. Then, too, she under-stands your taste, your likes and dislikes, and always knows exactly what to bring you to tempt your feeble appetite. Whoever heard of a nurse more fit for her work than Miss Nightingale? She seems as if God had sent her into the world on purpose, not only that she might be herself a nurse, but that she might teach others to nurse. It is even thus in spiritual things. I have used a homely illustration to show you what I mean. There are some people who, if they try to comfort the distressed, go to work so awkwardly that they are pretty sure to cause a great deal more trouble than they remove; to console the mourner is, evidently, not their *forte.* The true "help" to souls in trouble is one who, though his head may not be filled with classic lore, has a large and warm heart; he is, in fact, all heart. It was said of the beloved apostle John, that he was a pillar of fire from head to foot. This is the kind of man that a soul wants when it is shivering in the cold winter of despondency and distress. We know some such men; may God train many more, and give to all of us more of the gentleness that was in Christ; for, unless we are, in this way, fitted for the work, we shall never be able to do it properly.

A true "help" wants, not only a large and loving heart, but *a very quick eye and ear.* There is a way of getting the eye and ear sensitively acute with regard to sinners. I know some brethren and sisters who, when they are sitting in their pews, can almost tell how

the Word is operating upon those who are near them.
Trained and experienced "help" knows just what
they ought to say to their neighbours when the sermon
is over; they understand how to say it, and whether
they ought to say it in the pew, or going down the
stairs, or outside the building, or whether they ought
to wait till later in the week.   They have a kind of
sacred instinct; or, rather, an unction from the Holy
Spirit which tells them just what to do, how to do it,
and when to do it.   It is a blessed thing when God
thus sets His watchmen along the borders of the
Slough of Despond.   Then, with quick ears, they
listen to every sound; and, by-and-by, when they hear
a splash in any part of the mire, though it may be
very dark and misty, they hasten to the rescue.   Possibly, nobody else hears the cry of the soul in distress
but those who lay themselves out to listen for it.

We also want, for this work, men who are *swift of
foot,* to run to the relief of the distressed.   Some professors never speak to their neighbours about their
souls; but we thank God that there are others, who
will not let a stranger go away without an earnest
word concerning Christ.   I pray such "helps" to persevere in the good habit, and I am sure that the Lord
will bless them in it; for, while there is much that
can be done by the preacher who faithfully delivers his

Master's message, there is often even more that can be done by those who are able, in personal conversation, to get at the hearer's conscience, and, with the Holy Spirit's aid, to enlighten his soul.

For a thoroughly efficient "help", give us, also, *a man with a loving face.* We do not make our own faces; but no brother, who is habitually grim, will do much with anxious enquirers. Cheerfulness commends itself, especially to a troubled heart. We do not want levity in this holy service, but there is a great difference between cheerfulness and levity. I know that I can always tell what I feel to a man who looks kindly at me, but I could not communicate anything to one who, in a cold official way, talked at me from a great elevation, as though it were his business to enquire into my private concerns with the view of finding me out, and sending me to the rightabout. Engage in this difficult work softly, gently, affectionately; let your cheerful countenance tell that the religion you have is worth having, that it cheers and comforts you; for, in that way, the poor soul in the Slough of Despond will be more likely to hope that it will cheer and comfort him.

Earnestly, too, let me recommend you to have a *firm footing* if you mean to be a "help" to others. If you have to pull a brother out of the Slough, you must yourself stand fast; or, otherwise, while you are trying to lift him out, he may pull you into the mire. Recollect that, listening to the doubts of others may give rise to similar doubts in your own mind unless you are firmly established as to your own personal interest in Christ Jesus. If you would be useful in your Lord's service, you must not always be doubting and fearing. Full assurance is not necessary to salvation, but it is necessary to your success as a helper of others. I remember, when I first taught in a Sunday-school, that I was trying to point one of the boys in the class to the Saviour. He seemed troubled about his spiritual state, and he said to me, "Teacher, are you saved?" I replied, "Yes." "But are you sure you are?" he asked; and though I did not answer him just then, I felt that I could not very well assure him that there certainly was salvation in Jesus Christ, unless I had trusted Him myself, and proved His power to save. Endeavour to get a sure foothold yourself; for, then, you will be more useful around the edge of the Slough of Despond than those will be who are constantly slipping on its slimy banks.

As you want to help those who are struggling in the Slough, try to know it well; find out its worst parts, ascertain where it is deepest. You will not have to go far to learn this; you have probably been in it yourself, and therefore remember something about it; and you can easily gather from one and another whereabouts it is worst. Seek, if you can, to understand the mental philosophy of despondency of spirit; —I do not mean by studying Dugald Stewart and other writers on mental philosophy; but by real, heartfelt experience, seek to become practically acquainted with the doubts and fears which agitate awakened souls.

When you have done this, may the Lord give you— for you will need it if you are to become very useful,— *a strong hand,* in order that you may firmly grip the sinner whom you want to rescue! Our Lord Jesus Christ did not heal the lepers without touching them, and we cannot do good to our fellow-men if we always remain at a distance from them. The preacher is sometimes able to lay hold of his hearers; he can feel that he has them in his grasp, and that he can do almost anything he likes with them; and if you are to be a "help" to others, you will have to learn the blessed art of laying hold of the conscience, the heart, the judgment, the whole man. When you once get a grip of troubled heart, never let it go till you land it in peace. Have a hand like a vice, that will never let the sinner go when once you have hold of him. Shall a servant of God ever let a sinner fall back into the Slough when once he has taken him by the hand, and begun to pull him out? No; not while the rock, on which he stands, remains firm and steadfast, and he can hold the sinner by the hands of faith and prayer. May God teach you to clasp men by love, by spiritual sympathy, by that sacred passion for souls which will not let them go till they are saved!

Once more, if you would help others out of the Slough of Despond, you must have *a bending back.* You cannot draw them out if you stand bolt upright; you must go right down to where the poor creatures are sinking in the mire. They are almost gone; the mud and the slime are well-nigh over their heads; so you must roll up your sleeves, and go to work with a will if you mean to rescue them. "But they cannot speak correct English!" says someone. Never mind; do not speak superfine English to them, for they would not understand it; speak bad English which they can understand. It is said that many of the sermons of Augustine are full of shockingly bad Latin, not because Augustine was a poor Latin scholar, but because the dog-Latin of the day was better suited to the popular ear than more classically correct language would have been; and we shall have to speak in similar style if we want to get hold of men. There is a certain prudery about ministers which disqualifies them for

some kinds of work; they cannot bring their mouth
to utter the truth in such plain speech as fisher-women
would understand, but happy is that man whose mouth
is able to declare the truth in such a way that the persons to whom he is speaking will receive it. "But
remember the dignity of the pulpit," says one. Yes,
so I do; but what is that? The "dignity" of a war-
chariot consists in the number of captives that are
chained to its wheels, and "the dignity of the pulpit"
consists in the souls converted to God through the
Gospel proclaimed in it. Do not give your hearers any
sublime jargon, Johnsonian sentences, and rolling
periods; there is no "dignity" in any of these things
if they go over the heads of your hearers. You must,
as Paul wrote to the Romans, "condescend to men of
low estate;" and, sometimes, you will meet with men
and women whom you must address in a style which
does not commend itself to your own fastidious taste,
but which your judgment and your heart will command and compel you to use. Learn to stoop. Do not,
for instance, go into a cottage like a fine lady who
lets everybody see what a great thing it is for her to
condescend to visit poor people; go and sit down on
a broken chair, if there is no other in the room; sit on
the edge, if the rushes are gone; sit close to the good
woman, even if she is not as clean as she might be; and

talk to her, not as her superior, but as her equal. If there is a boy playing marbles, and you want to talk to him, you must not call him away from his play, nor look down upon him from a great elevation, as his schoolmaster might; but begin with a few playful expressions, and then drop a more serious sentence into his ear. If you would do people good, you must go down to them where they are. It is of no use to preach oratorical sermons to drowning men; you must go to the edge of the pool, stretch out your arms, and try to lay hold of them.

These, then, are some of the qualifications of a true "help."

Now I close by endeavoring to incite those of our brethren and sisters, who have been "helps" in the past, to go on yet more earnestly with that work in the future, and to stir up those who have not tried it, to begin at once.

Perhaps somebody asks, "Why should I help others?" My answer to that question is,—*because souls need help;* is not that enough? The cry of misery is a sufficient argument for the display of mercy. Souls are dying, perishing; therefore, help them. A few weeks ago, there was a story, in the papers, of a man being found dead in a ditch; and it was afterwards ascertained that he must have been lying there for six weeks. It was said that somebody had heard the cry, "Lost! Lost!" but it was dark, and he did not go out to see who it was! "Shocking! Shocking!" you say; and yet you may have acted in the very same way towards immortal souls. Among your neighbours, there are many who may not cry, "Lost!" because they do not feel that they are lost, yet they are; and will you let them die in the ditch of ignorance without going to their relief? There are others who are crying, "Lost!" and who need a word of comfort and direction; will you let them perish in despair for the want of it? Brethren and sisters in Christ, let the needs of humanity provoke you to activity on behalf of the many lost ones all around you.

Remember, also, *how you were yourselves helped when you were in a similar condition to theirs.* Some of us will never forget that dear Sunday-school teacher, that tender mother, that gracious woman, that kind young man, that excellent elder of the Church, who once did so much for us when we were in trouble of soul. We shall ever recollect their bright attention and assistance; they seemed to us like visions of bright angels when we were in the thick fog and darkness of despair. Then, repay the debt you owe to them, discharge the obligation by helping others as you were yourselves helped in your time of trouble.

Moreover, *Christ deserves it.* There is a lost lamb, out there in the darkness; it is His lamb, so will you not care for it for His sake? If there were a strange child at our door, asking for a night's shelter, common humanity might prompt us to take in the poor little creature out of the snow and wind; but if it were the child of our own brother, or of some dear friend, the sympathy of kinship would constrain us to protect it. That sinner is, in any case, your brother in the one great human family; so, by his relationship to you, though he may not discern it at present, a moral obligation rests upon you to give him all the help that is in your power.

Beloved, you would not want any other argument, did you know *how blessed the work is in itself.* Would you gain experience? Then, help others. Would you grow in grace? Then, help others. Would you shake off your own despondency? Then, help others. This work quickens the pulse, it clears the vision, it steels the soul to holy courage; it confers a thousand blessings on your own souls, to help others on the road to Heaven. Shut up your heart's floods, and they will become stagnant, noisome, putrid, foul; let them flow, and they shall be fresh and sweet, and shall well up continually. Live for others, and you will live a hundred lives in one. For true blessedness, divorce me from idleness, and unite me to industry.

If that is not sufficient reason, remember that *you are called to this work.* Your Master has hired you, so it is not your place to pick and choose what you will do. He has lent you your talents, so that you must do with them as he bids you. Determine that you will at once do some practical service for your Master, for He has called you to it. If you do not, you will probably soon feel the rod of correction. If you do not help others, God will treat you as men do their stewards who make no right use of the goods entrusted to them; your talent will be taken from you. Sickness may come upon you, because you were not active while you were in health; you may be reduced to poverty, because you did not make a right use of your riches; *you* may be brought into deep despair, because you have not helped despairing souls. Pharaoh's dream has often been fulfilled since his day. He dreamed that seven fat kine came up out of the river, and that there came up seven lean ones after them, and ate up the fat kine. Sometimes, when you are full of joy and peace, you are lazy and idle, and do no good to others; and when this is the case, you may well fear lest the seven lean kine should eat up the seven fat ones; and you may rest assured that lean days, in which you do nothing for your Master, lean Sundays, lean prayers, and so on, will eat up your fat Sabbaths, your fat graces, your fat joys, and then where will you be?

Besides all this, remember that, every hour we live, *we are getting nearer Heaven, and sinners are getting nearer hell.* The time in which we can serve Christ by winning souls is constantly waxing shorter. Our days are very few, so let us use them all for God. Let us not forget the reward which He will give to His faithful servants. Happy spirit, who shall hear others say, as he enters the celestial regions, "My father, I welcome thee!" Childless souls, in glory, who were never made a blessing to others on earth, must surely miss the very Heaven of Heaven; but they who have brought many to Christ shall have, in addition to their own bliss, the joy of sympathy with other spirits whom they were the means of leading to the Saviour. I wish I could put my Master's message into words that would burn their way into your hearts. I desire that every church-member may be a worker for Christ. We want no drones in this hive; and we want all bees, and no wasps. The most useless persons are generally the most quarrelsome; and those who are the most happy and peaceable, are usually those who are doing most for Christ. We are not saved by working, but by grace; but, because we are saved, we desire to be the instruments of bringing others to Jesus. I would stir you all up to help in this good work; old men, young men, brethren and sisters, according to your gifts and experience, help. I wish that each one of you would feel, "I cannot do much, but I can *help;* I cannot preach, but I can *help;* I cannot pray in public, but I can *help;* I cannot give much money away, but I can *help;* I cannot officiate as an elder or deacon, but I can *help;* I cannot shine as a 'bright particular star,' but I can *help;* I cannot stand alone to serve my Master, but I can *help.*" An old Puritan once preached a very singular sermon; there were only two words in the text, and they were, "and Bartholomew." The reason he took the text was, that, in the Gospel, Bartholomew's name is never mentioned alone; he is always associated with one of the other apostles. He is never the principal actor, but always second. Let this be your feeling; that, if you cannot do all yourself, you will *help* to do what you can.

When I gather my congregation together, I look upon the assembly as a meeting of council, to present degrees to such disciples as, through many sessions of labour, have merited them; and then I feel that we may confer upon those who have used the opportunities well, the sacred title of "Helps." Some of you have long earned this honorable name. Others of you shall have it when you deserve it; so make haste and win it. God grant that it may be your joy to enter Heaven, praising Him, that by His grace, He helped you to be a helper of others!

CHRISTIAN ENTERS THE WICKET GATE

V

CHRISTIAN AND THE ARROWS OF BEEL-ZEBUB.

"When Christian was stepping in at the Wicket Gate, Good-will gave him a pull. Then said Christian, 'What means that?' Good-will said to him, 'A little distance from this gate there is erected a strong castle, of which Beelzebub is the captain; from thence both he and them that are with him shoot arrows at those that come up to this gate, if haply they may die before they enter in.'

"Then said Christian, 'I rejoice and tremble.'"

IN this passage, Bunyan alludes to the fact that, when souls are just upon the verge of salvation, they are usually assailed by the most violent temptations. I may be addressing some who are just now in that condition. They are seeking the Saviour; they have begun to pray; they are anxious to believe on the Lord Jesus Christ; yet they are meeting with difficulties such as they never knew before, and they are almost at their wits' end. It may help them if we describe some of the arrows which were shot at us when we came to the gate, for it may be that the darts which are being shot at them are of a similar sort.

The most common one is this, *the fiery arrow of the remembrance of our sins.* "Ah!" saith the arch-enemy, "it is not possible that such sins as yours can be blotted out. Think of the number of your transgressions; how you have gone astray from your birth; how you have persevered in sin; how you have sinned against light and knowledge, against the most gracious invitations and the most terrible threatenings. You have done despite to the Spirit of Grace; you have trampled upon the blood of Christ; how can there be forgiveness for you?"

The stricken soul, crushed under a sense of sin, naturally endorses these insinuations. "It is true," says he, "though it is Satan who says it; I am just such a sinner as he describes." Then the poor soul fears whether pardon can be possible for such an offender; and, probably, he thinks of some gross sin that he has committed,—the blasphemer recollects his profanity, the unchaste man remembers his lasciviousness, and Satan whispers in his ear, "If thou hadst not committed that particular sin, there might have been hope for thee, but that transgression has carried thee over the verge of hope. Thou art now like the man in the iron cage; despair has laid hold of thee, and for thee there is now no deliverance." Poor heart! There are many passages of Scripture that ought to be sufficient to break or blunt all these fiery darts of the wicked one. These, for instance: "The blood of Jesus Christ His Son cleanseth us from all sin;" "All manner of sin and blasphemy shall be forgiven unto men;" "Him that cometh to Me I will in no wise cast out." God grant that they may be effective in your case!

Sometimes, another Satanic temptation strikes the sinner, like a bolt shot from an ancient cross-bow. It is this, *"It is too late for you to be saved.* You had many Gospel invitations when you were young; you were 'almost persuaded' while you were but a youth; but you halted so long between two opinions that, at last, the Lord lifted His hand, and sware in His wrath that you should not enter into His rest. You are, therefore, now past all hope." There are many who have been for years burdened with this terrible fear; and there are some, who seem to be like the prisoners in the condemned cell at Newgate, who could hear the big bell of St. Sepulchre's tolling their death-knell. Yet there is not a word of truth in these insinuations of Satan; for, as long as a man is in this world, if he doth but repent of sin, and believe in Jesus Christ, he shall be forgiven. There have been many sinners saved at the very end of their lives, as the penitent thief was. Many have been brought to Christ, and have been permitted to work in His vineyard even at the eleventh hour of the day. It is nowhere said, in

Scripture, that God will say to any man, who truly repents, that He will not receive him. There is no limitation of age in that text I quoted just now. "Him that cometh to Me I will in no wise cast out." If a man be ninety years of age, and he "cometh" to Christ, he shall not be cast out. Ay, and if he were as old as Methuselah, and he were to come to Christ, the promise would still hold good.

Where this fear vanishes, it is often followed by another. Satan says, "Yes, it may not be too late on account of your age, but *you have resisted the Holy Spirit; you have stifled conscience;* you have frequently, when you were 'almost persuaded,' said, 'Go thy way for this time; when I have a convenient season, I will send for thee.'" "Besides," the enemy may say, "you were once outwardly so religious that everybody thought you were a Christian, and you even thought so yourself. You used to teach in the Sunday-school, and you sometimes preached; but you know where you have been, and how you have acted, since then. You have returned, like the dog to his vomit, and like the sow that was washed to her wallowing in the mire; so, now, there can be no hope for you. You may knock at Mercy's gate, but it will not open to you." Now, dear friends, sharp as that arrow is, and well aimed as it frequently is, there is no real force in it. If Christ never received those who have once rejected Him, He would never have received any of us, for some of us refused His invitations, and stifled the admonitions of conscience a thousand times, yet, when we came to Jesus, He received us graciously, and loved us freely. Yes, beloved, and if you come to Him after you have rejected ten thousand invitations, if you trust in Him after all your thwartings of the Spirit of God, you shall in no wise be cast out.

Many burdened souls have been greatly troubled concerning *the doctrine of election.* It is part of the craft of Satan to take a truth which is more precious than fine gold, and to turn it into a stumbling-block in the way of a sinner who is coming to Christ. The doctrine of election is like a diamond for brilliance; but the devil knows how to use its sharp edge to the grievous wounding of many a poor sinner. "You are not elect," says Satan; "you were never chosen by God: your name is not in the Lamb's Book of Life." How easily the sinner might answer the accuser if he were but in his wits! He might say, "How do you know that I am not elect, and that my name is not in the Book of Life? God has never authorized you to convey to me this doleful news, therefore I shall not distress myself about it." Why should we let such a fear as this keep us from Christ, when we do not let it keep us from other actions? A man is very ill, and his wife says that she will fetch a physician. "No, my dear wife," says he, "it is no use fetching a physician, for I am afraid I am predestined to die." Here is a man who is travelling, and suddenly he meets with an accident. Of course, he endeavours to extricate himself; but if he were to talk, as some do in spiritual matters, he would say, "I do not know whether I am ordained to escape, and therefore I shall not try." Does a shipwrecked sailor give up swimming because he does not know whether he will ever reach the land? Do you give up working because you do not know whether you will get your wages? Do you cease eating because you do not know whether you are ordained to live another day? Do you refuse to go to sleep because you do not know whether it is decreed that you are to wake any more? Nay, but you go about the affairs of life independently of any thoughts about the Divine decree, and in that way the Divine decree is realized in you. You are bidden, in God's Word, to believe in the Lord Jesus Christ; and I will tell you one thing, that is, if you do believe in Christ, that is proof positive that you are one of the elect, and that your name is in the Book of Life. I have never seen that Book, but I know that no soul ever did believe in Jesus whose name was not already recorded there. If thou comest to Christ, repenting of thy sin, I know that God has chosen thee unto eternal life, for repentance is God's gift, and it is a token of His everlasting love. He says, "I have loved thee with an everlasting love : therefore with loving kindness have I drawn thee." God draws us to repentance and faith by the bands of His love because He has loved us from eternity. So, let not that blessed word "election" ever trouble you. The day will come when you will dance at the very sound of it; and, then, nothing will fill your heart with such music as the thought that the Lord has chosen you from before the foundation of the world to be the object of His special grace.

Another of the devil's fiery darts is this, *"You have committed the unpardonable sin."* Ah! this arrow has rankled in many a heart, and it is very difficult to deal with such cases. The only way in which I argue with a person thus assailed is to say, "I am quite certain that, if you desire salvation, you have not committed the unpardonable sin, and I am absolutely sure that, if you will now come and trust Christ, you have not committed that sin, for every soul that trusts Christ is forgiven, according to God's Word, and therefore you cannot have committed that sin." Nobody knows what that sin is. I believe that even

God's Word does not tell us, and it is very proper
that it does not. As I have often said, it is like the
notice we sometimes see put up, "Man-traps and spring
gun set here." We do not know whereabouts the
traps and guns are, but we have no business over the
hedge at all. So, "there is a sin unto death;" we are
not told what that sin is, but we have no business to
go over the hedge into any transgression at all. That
"sin unto death" may be different in different people;
but, whoever commits it, from that very moment, loses
all spiritual desires. He has no wish to be saved, no
care to repent, no longing after Christ; so dreadful
is the spiritual death that comes over the man who
has committed it that he never craves eternal life. We
need not pray for such a case as that; the apostle John
says, "I do not say that he shall pray for it." I have
met with some few cases, in which there has been such
stolid indifference to all Divine things, or such jeering,
mocking scorn at everything spiritual that, though I
would pray for the very worst of sinners, I have felt,
"I cannot pray for that man." But none of you are in
that condition if you long for mercy; if you hate sin,
and seek to escape from it, that sin unto death has
not been committed by you.

There are others who are troubled with this temptation, that *it would be presumption for them to trust*

Christ. That is another of Satan's lies, for it can never be presumption for a man to do what the Word of God tells him to do. If the Lord Jesus Christ bids a man trust Him, it must be the man's duty to do so; and, consequently, it cannot be presumption. It *is* presumption to say, "O Lord, Thou hast bidden me trust Thee, but I am afraid that I may not." That is presumption of the worst possible kind. "I cannot repent as I would," says one. Who made you a judge of your own repentance? You are told to trust in what Christ has done. "But I cannot pray as I should like to do." Who told you that you were to trust in your prayers? You are to rely on what Christ has done for you, and not on what you can do for yourself. "But if I could get into a better state of mind, I should have hope." Who told you that you were to get into a better state of mind, and then come to Christ? The Gospel message is: "Come just as you are, poor sinner, and cast yourself upon Christ, resting entirely upon the person, the blood, the righteousness of the once-crucified but now exalted Redeemer." It is no presumption for thee to do this. Nobody ever did get to Heaven by presumption, but unnumbered millions have entered there by trusting Christ, and you will be one of them if you will but trust in Him, and in Him alone.

Besides all these fiery darts that I have mentioned, there are many indefinable insinuations which Satan casts into the hearts of men when they are coming to Christ. I should hardly like to tell you what they are; for I might, by so doing, really do the devil's work; but this one may serve as a specimen. Men, and women, too, have sometimes been in such trouble of soul that *they have been tempted to self-destruction.* There have been instances in which they have almost committed that awful crime; but, just at the last, there has been some Good-will to stretch out his hand, and pull them inside the door of mercy. "Ah!" thinks Satan, "if I could only get one of God's elect people to destroy himself before he believed in Jesus, I should be able to boast of it forever." Ay, but he never has done that, and he never will. If thou, my friend, shouldst ever be tempted to commit that sin, thou mayest well say, "What good could I get by destroying myself? What! 'Leap out of the frying-pan into the fire,' as the old proverb says. To escape from my sins, I shall rush, red-handed, before my Maker's bar?" There is no insanity like that. Art thou in such dreadful haste to die, and in such a hurry to surround thyself with quenchless flames? Oh, think not of it; but turn to Jesus, for there is hope yet, even for thee, and if thou wilt but cast thyself upon Him, thou shalt have joy and peace in believing.

VI.

CHRISTIAN AT THE CROSS.

"Now I saw in my dream that the highway, up which Christian was to go, was fenced on either side with a wall, and that wall was called Salvation. Up this way therefore did burdened Christian run, but not without great difficulty because of the load on his back. He ran thus till he came to a place somewhat ascending, and upon that place stood a cross, and a little below in the bottom a sepulchre."

A VOICE said "Away, away to Calvary!" Yet he trembled at the voice, for he said within himself, "Why should I go thither, for there my blackest sin was committed; there I murdered the Saviour by my transgressions." But Mercy beckoned and said, "Come, come away, poor sinner!" And the sinner followed. The chains were on his legs and hands, but he crept as best he could, till he came to the foot of the hill called Calvary, on the summit of which he saw a cross. O sinner, I would that thou wouldst stand at the foot of the cross, and think of Jesus till thou couldst find comfort! I believe the shortest way to faith is to consider well the object of faith. The true way to get comfort is not to try to comfort yourself away from the cross, but think of

Christ dying for you till you are comforted; say unto your soul, "I will never remove from the cross until I am washed in this precious blood:

> " 'Blest Saviour, at Thy feet I lie,
> Here to receive a cure or die;
> But grace forbids that painful fear,
> Almighty grace, which triumphs here.' "

Healing came to the sin-bitten by looking at the serpent, not by looking at their own wounds, nor yet by hearing about the cure of others; and, even so, healing will come to you, not by looking at sin, nor hearing about Christ, so much as by fixing your mind's eye upon the cross, and meditating upon Him who died thereon, till, as by considering His merits, you believe on Him, and so are saved.

"So I saw in my dream, that just as Christian came up with the cross, his burden loosed from off his shoulders, and fell from off his back, and began to tumble, and so continued to do till it came to the mouth of the sepulchre, where it fell in, and I saw it no more."

The Pilgrim was never eased of his burden till he came to the foot of the cross, and there he lost it for ever. Bunyan did not intend by this the Popish symbol which is now so commonly had in reverence; he had no respect for such baubles and idolatries. He meant that a burdened soul finds no peace until it trusts in the atoning Sacrifice of Jesus. Sin must be punished; conscience knows this, and makes the sinner tremble. Jesus was punished in the stead of those who trust Him, the believer knows this, and feels that he is justly secure from further penalty; his conscience rests, and his heart is glad. If Jesus bore the penalty of the law for me, then God is just, and yet I am safe. Two punishments for one offence cannot be demanded by justice; a suffering Jesus prevents the possibility of those being condemned for whom He died as a substitute. In the wounds of Jesus there is rest for the weary consciences, but nowhere else. They who trust in the merit of His atonement are saved from wrath through Him. When Dr. Neale, the eminent ritualist, Romanized "Pilgrim's Progress," he represented the pilgrim as coming to a certain bath, into which he was plunged, and *there* his burden was washed away. According to this doctored edition of the allegory, Christian was washed in the laver of baptism, and all his sins were thus removed. That is the High Church mode of getting rid of sin. The true way is to lose it at the cross. Now, mark what happened. According to Dr. Neale's "Pilgrim's Progress," that burden grew again on the pilgrim's back. I do not wonder at that; for a burden which baptism can remove is sure to come again, but the burden which is lost at the cross never appears again for ever.

"Then was Christian glad and lightsome, and said with a merry heart, He hath given me rest by His sorrow, and life by His death. Then he stood awhile to look and wonder, for it was very surprising to him that the sight of the cross should thus ease him of his burden. He looked, therefore, and looked again, even till the springs that were in his head sent the waters down his cheeks."

Let awakened sinners beware of receiving comfort from those who depreciate repentance. It is after all no little thing. They tell us "It is only a change of mind." But what a change of mind! The words sound little enough, but repentance itself is no trifle. They tell us that repentance does not necessarily imply sorrow for sin; but we solemnly warn them, and all others whom it may concern, that if their repentance has in it no grief for having offended, it is not repentance after a godly sort, and will need to be repented of. A dry-eyed repentance is no repentance. They who turn unto the Lord aright, mourn for sin and are in bitterness as one that is in bitterness for his first-born. It is from the cross that both repentance and faith arise. We do not bring these graces to the cross, but find them at the cross. They are love-tokens from Jesus. When He arises in us as the Sun of Righteousness, these are His early beams. Oh, that all poor sinners would come and sit in this sunshine.

When I think of my transgressions, better known to myself than to anyone else, and remember too that they are not known even to me as they are to God, I feel all hope swept away and my soul left in utter despair, until I come anew to the cross, and bethink me of who it was that died there, and what designs of infinite mercy are answered by His death. It is so sweet to look up at the Crucified One again, and say, "I have nought but Thee, my Lord, no confidence but Thee. If Thou be not accepted as my substitute I must perish, if God's appointed Saviour be not enough I have no other, but I know thou art the Father's well-beloved, and I am accepted in Thee. Thou art all I have, or want."

Beloved, I think that you know, in your own experience, that it was Christ's death that really operated most upon you in the matter of your conversion. I hear much talk about the example of Christ having great effect upon ungodly men; but I do not believe it, and certainly have never seen it. It has great effect upon men when they are born again, and are saved from the wrath to come, and are full of gratitude on this account; but before that happens, we have known men to admire the conduct of Christ, and even write books about the beauty of His character, while, at the same time, they have denied His Godhead. Thus they have rejected Him in His essential character, and there has been no effect produced upon their conduct by their cold admiration of His life. But when a man comes to see that he is pardoned and saved through the death of Jesus, he is moved to gratitude, and then to love. "We love Him because He first loved us." That love which He displayed in His death has touched the mainspring of our being, and moved us with a passion to which we were strangers before; and, because of this, we hate the sins that once were sweet, and turn with all our hearts to the obedience that once was so unpleasant. There is more effect in faith in the blood of Christ to change the human character than in every other consideration. The cross once seen, sin is crucified: the passion of the Master once apprehended as being endured for us, we then feel that we are not our own, but are bought with a price. This perception of redeeming love, in the death of our Lord Jesus, makes all the difference: this prepares us for a higher and a better life than we have ever known before. It is His death that does it.

"Now, as he stood looking and weeping, behold three shining ones came to him, and saluted him with 'Peace be to thee.'

So the first said to him, 'Thy sins be forgiven;' the second stripped him of his rags, and clothed him with change of raiment; the third also set a mark upon his forehead, and gave him a roll with a seal upon it, which he bid him look on as he ran, and that he should give it in at the celestial gate; so they went their way. Then Christian gave three leaps for joy, and went on singing:—

> "'Thus far did come loaden with my sin,
> Nor could aught ease the grief that I was in,
> Till I came hither: what a place is this!
> Must here be the beginning of my bliss?
> Must here the burden fall from off my back?
> Must here the strings that bound it to me crack?
> Blest Cross! blest sepulchre, blest rather be
> The Man that there was put to shame for me!'"

Imagine the experience of some dear friend, who has just believed in Jesus, and to whom the Spirit of God bears witness that he is forgiven. What sort of a man will he be? I will try to picture him to you. Already I see his eyes glistening with a light I never saw there before. The man looks positively handsome; you would hardly recognize him if you knew him before this great change happened to him. He had a burden on his mind that made him always look careworn. That has gone, and now he looks supremely blest. But I also see tears in his eyes; how came they there? He was not much given to weeping in his old days? He is grieving to think that he should ever have offended so kind a God; for nothing makes us so sorry for sin as the sense of being completely forgiven. He knows he is pardoned, he is sure of it;

he knows that God loves him, and now he loathes himself that he should ever have sunk so low. Yet, if you will take one of his tears, and put it under a microscope, or analyze its component parts, you will find that there is no bitterness in it. Joy is mingled with his sorrow as he stands at the foot of the cross, and bathes his Lord's feet with his penitential yet rainbowed tears. Now see him go home. He has some Christian friends there, I hope; and if so, he will not be long with them before they begin to notice the change in him, and he is not long before he wants to tell them the blessed secret. Mother wants to know what has happened to her boy, and his arms are thrown around her neck as he says, "Mother, I have found the Lord." She is very delighted, and perhaps very surprised, for it was not his usual way to talk about religion; he used sometimes to sneer and jeer at it. Will he go to bed without prayer? No; he needs nobody to tell him to pray; he has been praying all the way home, and while he has been sitting there. These are the first real prayers he has ever presented; but it has now become as natural for him to pray as it is for a living man to breathe.

The time when Christians begin to sing in the ways of the Lord is when they first lose their burden at the foot of the Cross. Not even the songs of the angels

seem so sweet as the first song of rapture which gushes
from the inmost soul of the forgiven child of God.
Well might poor Pilgrim, having lost his load, give
three great leaps for joy and go on singing:—

"Blest Cross! blest sepulchre! blest rather be
  The Man that there was put to shame for me!"

Believer, do you recollect the day when your fetters
fell off? Do you remember the place where Jesus met
you and said, "I have loved thee with an everlasting
love; I have blotted out as a cloud thy transgressions,
and as a thick cloud thy sins; they shall not be mentioned against thee any more for ever?" Oh! what
a sweet season is that when Jesus takes away the pain
of sin. When the Lord first pardoned my sin, I was
so joyous that I could scarce refrain from dancing.
I thought on my road home from the house where I
had been set at liberty, that I must tell the stones in
the street the story of my deliverance. So full was
my soul of joy, that I wanted to tell every snowflake
that was falling from the Heaven of the wondrous love
of Jesus, who had blotted out the sins of one of the
chief of rebels. That happy day, when I found the
Saviour and learned to cling to His dear feet, was a
day never to be forgotten by me. I can testify that
the joy of that day was utterly indescribable. There
was no expression, however fanatical, which would

have been out of keeping with the joy of my spirit at that hour.   Many days of Christian experience have passed since then, but there has never been one which has had the full exhilaration, the sparkling delight which that first day had.   I thought I could have sprung from the seat on which I sat, and have called out with the wildest of those Methodist brethren who were present, "I am forgiven!   I am forgiven!   A monument of grace!   A sinner saved by blood."   My spirit saw its chains broken to pieces, I felt that I was an emancipated soul, an heir of heaven, a forgiven one, accepted in Jesus, plucked out of the miry clay and out of the horrible pit, with my feet set upon a rock, and my goings established.   I could understand what John Bunyan meant, when he declared that he wanted to tell the crows on the ploughed land all about his conversion.

I have heard a Christian say that when he found the Saviour he was so happy that he did not know how to contain himself, and he sang like a whole band of music,

> "Happy day, happy day,
> When Jesus washed my sins away."

It is the privilege of true believers to be "singing all the time."   Joy in God is suitable to our condition.

"Why should the children of a King
    Go mourning all their days?"

Joy in the Lord is more injurious to Satan's empire than anything. I am of the same mind as Luther, who, when he heard any bad news, used to say, "Come, let us sing a psalm, and spite the devil."

"They shall sing in the ways of the Lord." When the ways get very rough, and become the paths of suffering, and the pains are frequent and intense, sing still. No music that goes up to the throne of God is sweeter in Jehovah's ear than the song of suffering saints. They shall bless Him upon their beds and sing His high praises in the fire. To go right through the Valley of the Shadow of Death, and sing all the way; to climb the Hill Difficulty, and to sing up its crags; to pass by Giant Grim, and even by the Castle of Giant Despair, and through the Enchanted Ground and still to keep singing, and to come to the river's brink and descend into it still singing—this is lovely in a Christian. May the statutes of the Lord be our songs in the house of our pilgrimage, till we mount to sing above!

We owe all to Jesus crucified. What is your life, my brethren, but the cross? Whence comes the bread of your soul but from the cross? What is your joy but the cross? What is your delight, what is your heaven, but the Blessed One, once crucified for you, who ever liveth to make intercession for you? Cling to the cross, then. Put both arms around it! Hold to the Crucified, and never let Him go. Come afresh to the cross at this moment, and rest there now and for ever! Then, with the power of God resting upon you, go forth and preach the cross! Tell out the story of the bleeding Lamb. Repeat the wondrous tale, and nothing else. Never mind how you do it, only proclaim that Jesus died for sinners. The cross held up by a babe's hand is just as powerful as if a giant held it up. The power lies in the word itself, or rather in the Holy Spirit who works by it and with it.

O glorious Christ, when I have had a vision of Thy cross, I have seen it at first like a common gibbet, and Thou wast hanging on it like a felon; but, as I have looked, I have seen it begin to rise, and tower aloft till it has reached the highest heaven, and by its mighty power has lifted up myriads to the throne of God. I have seen its arms extend and expand until they have embraced all the earth. I have seen the foot of it go down deep as our helpless miseries are; and what a vision I have had of Thy magnificence, O Thou crucified One!

Brethren, believe in the power of the cross for the conversion of those around you. Do not say of any man that he cannot be saved. The blood of Jesus is omnipotent. Do not say of any district that it is too sunken, or of any class of men that they are too far gone: the word of the cross reclaims the lost. Believe it to be the power of God, and you shall find it so. Believe in Christ crucified, and preach boldly in His name, and you shall see great and gladsome things. Do not doubt the ultimate triumph of Christianity. Do not let a mistrust flit across your soul. The cross must conquer; it must blossom with a crown, a crown commensurate with the person of the Crucified, and the bitterness of His agony. His reward shall parallel His sorrows. Trust in God, and lift your banner high, and now with psalms and songs advance to battle, for the Lord of hosts is with us, the Son of the Highest leads our van. Onward, with blast of silver trumpet and shout of those that seize the spoil. Let no man's heart fail him! Christ hath died! Atonement is complete! God is satisfied! Peace is proclaimed! Heaven glitters with proofs of mercy already bestowed upon ten thousand times ten thousand! Hell is trembling, heaven adoring, earth waiting. Advance, ye saints, to certain victory! You shall overcome through the blood of the Lamb.

FORMALIST   HYPOCRISY

VII.
FORMALIST AND HYPOCRISY.

"Christian espied two men come tumbling over the wall, on the left hand of the narrow way; and they made up apace to him. The name of the one was Formalist, and the name of the other Hypocrisy. So, as I said, they drew up unto him, who thus entered with them into discourse:—

"CHR. Gentlemen, whence came you, and whither do you go?

"FORM. and HYP. We were born in the land of Vainglory, and are going for praise to Mount Sion.

"CHR. Why came you not in at the gate which standeth at the beginning of the way? Know you not that it is written, that he that cometh not in by the door, 'but climbeth up some other way, the same is a thief and a robber'? (John x. i.

"They said that, to go to the gate for entrance was, by all their countrymen, counted too far about; and that, therefore, their usual way was to make a short cut of it, and to climb over the wall, as they had done.

"CHR. But will it not be counted a trespass against the Lord of the city whither we are bound, thus to violate His revealed will?

"They told him that, as for that, he needed not to trouble his head thereabout; for what they did, they had custom for; and could produce, if need were, testimony that would witness it for more than a thousand years."

AFTER Christian had been at the foot of the cross, and had been stripped of his rags, and had received a change of raiment, and a mark in his forehead, and a roll with a seal upon it, he went on his way rejoicing. He had not gone far before he came to three men fast asleep, with fetters upon their heels. These were Simple, Sloth, and Presumption. Christian woke them, and offered to help them off with their irons; but they soon lay down again, and he had to go on alone. While he was troubled in his mind by their indifference, "he espied two men come tumbling over the wall, on the left hand of the narrow way." Possibly, there had been some revival services, and at an exciting meeting these two men had, all of a sudden, determined to be Christians. They did not take the trouble to obtain true repentance and a living faith in the crucified Saviour. They did not care about real heart work, nor about the operations of the Holy Spirit within them; but they resolved to make a profession of being Christians, and to join the church. They thought that, as Christians wore a certain style of coat, they would wear the same, but they were not concerned as to whether their hearts were right with God or not. They came tumbling over the wall.

Bunyan says "they made up apace" to Christian. It had taken him a long time to get where he was, but they caught up with him in a minute or two. None seemed to grow so rapidly as those who have no roots, and who therefore are not really growing at all. A child, with a farthing's worth of soap and a pipe, soon blows some big bubbles, painted with many colours and sparkling with beauty; but they are only bubbles. They are very quickly produced, and they as speedily vanish. Beware of getting up a sham religion. You can easily paint and grain a piece of common wood so that it will be taken for oak or sandal-wood; but it would take many years to grow the genuine oak, and many months to bring the sandal-wood from the far-off land. To imitate a good thing may be rapid work, but it will not last. You who catch up so soon with older Christians, mind that yours is personal experience, and not such as is learned from books, or picked up at an experience meeting. When a man has nothing to carry, he can run quickly. Empty drums make a great sound, and brooks that are shallow flow at a great rate. So the Formalist and Hypocrisy make up apace to Christian.

I do not know to what sect Formalist belonged. I know his father very well, and he had several children. One of them used to go to the Church of England; in fact, two or three of that branch of the family, who were very happy and comfortable, always attended there. One or two of them took to going a little further than the Church of England, and made towards Rome, multiplying ceremonies, and gaudy dresses, and I know not what besides. But, if I recollect right, there was one of the sons who was a Presbyterian;—he could not bear anything like Romanism, but he was a great stickler for all the forms of the kirk nevertheless. Another of the sons joined the Baptists, and a mighty fine fellow he was,—as orthodox as possible. He knew what was what in doctrine, and demanded sixteen ounces to the pound, and a little over. He would fight tooth and nail for the defence of believers' baptism and the Lord's Supper. I am not quite certain, but I sometimes fear that at least one of the Formalist family is a member at the Tabernacle. If it is not one of the sons, perhaps it is a grandson who comes here. There are many of these people about, and we must not be surprised if some of them come to us.

"Oh!" say they, "we will try to be Christians; and, in order to be Christians, there are such-and-such outward actions to be performed. We will attend the prayer-meeting; we will go to the Bible-classes; we will see the elders; we will be baptized; we will join the church; and when we have done all this, we shall have got into the right road, certainly. Have we not received, as it were, the certificate of God's own Church that we are all right? It is true that we have tumbled over the wall; we have not been humbled on account of sin; we have not put our trust in the Lord Jesus Christ; still, we are in the right way; does not everybody say that we are? Therefore, all must be well with us." Such was Formalist.

Hypocrisy, however, was the bigger rogue of the two, for he had not any belief in the matter at all. Formalist had, perhaps, some measure of faith of a certain sort; he thought there might be something in forms and ceremonies. But Hypocrisy said in his heart, "Ah! it is all a pretty story, but then it is a very respectable story; and if I pretend to believe it, people will think the better of me." I recollect one member of this family saying, "If I join the church, possibly I may get an almshouse;" and another reflected, "Very likely I might secure a pension of so much a week." Another thought, "It would be a capital thing to get into the ministry, and pick up a good living that way." And another said within himself, "This would increase my trade; people would say, 'He goes to such-and-such a chapel, we must deal with him, you know.'"

There is a very numerous family of this class; and there are some others who do not expect, perhaps, to get any pecuniary gain by professing to be Christians, but who feel, "Well, you see, it makes you seem to be a good sort of person, you get the respect and esteem of your friends; your mother will be pleased; your husband will be glad; all your friends will feel so satisfied, and they will make quite a fuss over you." So the man goes in for it, though, in his heart, he says, "There is nothing in it; it is all rubbish." He tumbles over the wall; he does not care about the secret power of vital godliness. It is enough for him that he has got into the Christian Church, and there he means to stick. He sometimes says that he is as good as the most of us; and though he knows he is as rotten as he can be, yet he boasts himself above those trembling but earnest souls who cannot talk so glibly, nor fly so many colours at their masthead.

Well, these two men drew up apace to Christian, and he saluted them, for it is not the Christian's duty to suspect anybody; and when he finds people in the right road, he must treat them as if they were sincere until he has proof to the contrary. If it is the law of England that every man is to be accounted honest, till he is proved to be a rogue, it should certainly be the law of the Christian Church. So, seeing them in the narrow road, in which there are so few travellers, Christian began to speak with them. He asked them whence they came, and they answered, "We were born in the land of Vain-glory." That is where all formalists and hypocrites come from. They glory in themselves. They think their own hearts are right. They conclude that their natural goodness suffices, and therefore a few forms and a bare profession will serve them in the day of judgment. Christian also asked them, "Whither go you?" "We are going," they said, "for praise to Mount Sion." Alas, for love of praise! It is a most damnable snare. We all love praise; it is useless to deny it. It has been said that—

"The proud, to gain it, toils on toils endure;
The modest shun it but to make it sure."

We all have an eye to it at times, and no man can say that he does not more or less desire it. Of course, we do not like flattery when it is laid on with a trowel. We do not want great lumps of butter on our bread, for then we begin to suspect that it is not genuine. All of us are capable of receiving a goodly amount of praise, but it is difficult to remain in a healthy state under such circumstances.

These two men were seeking after praise. They loved the praise of men more than the praise of God. Brethren, do not we sometimes do good actions out of a desire for praise? I was thinking about this very matter to-day. I have undertaken a certain duty which I do not particularly like. I would get out of it if I dared, for I do not think I shall succeed in it, and it will occupy much of my time, and give me a deal of trouble. But, while I was murmuring to myself about what a stupid I was to venture on so ungrateful a task, I thought, "I shall receive no honour and no credit for it; but, still, if I do it with a view to God's glory throughout, and with no consideration for myself, that is enough." If I take up a difficult work that I like, and succeed in it, everybody will say, "He has done it thoroughly well," and so I get praise here, though I may not hear the "Well done!" when I get to my Master at the last. But if I undertake anything from which the flesh shrinks, with a single eye to God's glory, I shall have the sweet satisfaction that my Lord approves of my action whatever comes of it. Take care, I pray you, of "going for praise to Mount Sion."

Christian next asked these two men this very important question, "Why came you not in at the gate which standeth at the beginning of the way?" Now, if there should be anybody here who is saying to himself, "I am all right; I have always attended my parish church, or I have always gone to the meeting-house," if there is one here who says, "I am all right, for I was christened," or "I am all right, for I was baptized," I ask you, "Why came you not in at the

gate which standeth at the beginning of the way?"
How is it that you did not come as God has bidden
you come, by a living faith in the living Saviour; by
repentance; by reliance upon Him who alone is the
Way, the Truth, and the Life? If you have been a
church-member no matter how many years, better
give up that position than let a religious profession
be a winding-sheet in which to envelop a corpse. Have
the life Divine within you, or else, in the Name of
God, I beseech you not to make a profession which
you cannot by any possibility adorn, but which will
be the ruin of the your soul at the last!

In answer to Christian's question, "Why came you
not in at the gate?" Formalist and Hypocrisy gave a
reason which seemed to them sufficient. "They said
that, to go to the gate for entrance was, by all their
countrymen, counted too far about; and that, therefore, their usual way was to make a short cut of it,
and to climb over the wall, as they had done."
Formalists think, "We do not mind being christened,
confirmed, taking the sacrament, and going to church
or chapel; but this repenting of sin, this believing,
this clinging to Christ, this seeking after holiness,—
ah! 'it is too far about.'" They would rather tumble
over the wall. They cry, "Peace, peace; when there
is no peace." I hope you, dear friends, are not so

foolish as that. Better go never so far roundabout, and be right, than jump hastily at a false conclusion, and find yourself mistaken. Besides, it is not "far about," after all. The safe way is really a short way, and to trust in Christ is the direct road to eternal life.

Christian further very properly asked these men how, if it was a trespass against God to get into the road without coming in at the gate, they hoped to be accepted. If, without faith, it is impossible to please God, how can you expect to please Him by trusting to forms and ceremonies? Even your prayers are an abomination unto God unless you have come to Him, through Christ, for mercy and forgiveness. If you rest in your Bible-reading, or your chapel-going, or your Sunday-school teaching,—if you depend upon anything that you are, or do, or feel, you are leaning upon that which will fail you at the last. You are really making an anti-Christ of these things, and putting them into the place of Jesus. How can you be right at the end if you are wrong at the start? If you come not in at the door, rest assured that you will never reach the gates of Paradise.

These men told Christian that "he needed not to trouble his head thereabout;" and that is the answer of many formalists and hypocrites. They are harder to deal with than are the professedly unconverted.

Those who have no sense of religion at all will often listen to what you have to say; while those other people, who know so much, and practise so little, tell you to mind your own business, for they are as good as you are. If you ever talk to a genuine Christian in that way, he is very thankful to you for the exhortation to examine himself. The true child of God, when he is under a searching ministry, will bear the wound, and will ask God to help the minister to probe it. It is a sign of a good state of heart when you are willing to be probed; but it is a terrible proof of hypocrisy and formalism when you say to others, "Let each man keep to his own religion; you go your way, and leave me to mine; I daresay I am as right as you are."

These men further assured Christian that it had been the custom for more than a thousand years. In that, they spoke truly. Men have relied on outward forms, and thought themselves something when they were nothing, from time immemorial. One who walked with Christ, and who even ate the sop out of the same dish with Him, betrayed Him. There have always been some having a form of godliness, but denying the power thereof. Such were "spots" in the solemn feasts of apostolic days. They were "clouds without water, trees without fruit, twice dead, plucked up by the roots." It is so still. There are, indeed, most venerable precedents for formalism and hypocrisy. Go to Rome, and you will see plenty of them. Go into a large number of our parish churches in England, and you will see formality run mad. Step into our own Dissenting places of worship, and even in our decent sobriety how much there may be of dead formalism! Alas! this is the religion of many professing Christians all through the land, "You need not trouble about faith, or those other weighty matters which concern the soul and God; but if you go to your place of worship, and take your seat there regularly, all will be well with you." This is false religion; may God save us from it! May we be sincere, in our love to Christ, and in our faith in His atoning sacrifice!

VIII.

FORMALIST AND HYPOCRISY.
Concluded.

" 'But,' said Christian, 'will your practice stand a trial at law?' "

I LIKE Christian's way of bringing the matter in dispute to a test; and I desire to pass on, to each one of you, the question that he put to Formalist and Hypocrisy, "Will your practice stand a trial at law?" Blessed be God, if we are relying on the Lord Jesus Christ, we need not fear the result of any trial at law. It is according to the law, surely, that a man should keep his promise, and that an oath should be binding upon him who takes it; and we have these "two immutable things in which it was impossible for God to lie,"—namely, His promise and His oath,— "that we might have a strong consolation, who have fled for refuge to lay hold upon the hope set before us."

"God has promised to forgive
All who on His Son believe;"—

and that is a matter which will stand a trial at law. If we believe on Him, He must and will forgive us.

The two men could not answer that straight question, so they said to Christian, "If we get into the way, what matter which way we get in? If we are in, we are in; thou art but in the way, who, as we perceive, came in at the gate; and we are also in the way, that came tumbling over the wall." So, many say, nowadays, "You are professors, and we are professors; you come to the Lord's Supper, and we come to the Lord's Supper; you are a Christian, and we are Christians; one is as good as another, you know; and every tub stands on its own bottom." These people declare that they are just as good as you Christians are, and I have sometimes known Formalist to say, "I am a great deal better than you are, for you often have to complain that your life is not up to the mark that you know you ought to reach. I have heard you confess, in your prayers, that you are far from perfect. Now, I *am* perfect." Have you never heard Formalist talk like that? I have, many a time. I have known persons come to join the church, who, in answer to my questions, have told me that they were perfect. One man assured me that he had lived for six months without sin in thought, and word, and deed. I asked him if he was sure of that, and he replied, "Yes." "Well, then," I answered, "I cannot propose you for membership in this church, because there is nobody else of that sort amongst us, and I am afraid that you would be unhappy amongst such poor imperfect creatures as we are." So I sent him on his way.

There are others, who are not such fools as to claim absolute perfection, but they think that they are marvelously near it. I was amused, to-day, when I read an advertisement of "an ivory church-service, with gilt edges, and lined with satin." That is for the use of "miserable sinners" on Sundays! It seemed odd to me; yet how much of our religion is just like it! It is very fine work for those who dwell in dust and ashes. There is much of pride even in our humility.

When Formalist and Hypocrisy said to Christian, "We see not wherein thou differest from us, but by the coat that is on thy back, which was, as we trow, given thee by some of thy neighbours, to hide the shame of thy nakedness," the true pilgrim made a most suitable reply. He said:—

" 'It was given me by the Lord of the place whither I go; and that, as you say, to cover my nakedness with. And I take it as a token of His kindness to me; for I had nothing but rags before. And, besides, thus I comfort myself as I go: Surely, think I, when I come to the gate of the city, the Lord thereof will know me for good, since I have His coat on my back,—a coat that He gave me freely in the day that He stripped me of my rags.' "

This is one of the things that the formalist cannot

imitate,—the robe of Christ's righteousness, accompanied by a humble sense of one's own unrighteousness and raggedness. The hypocrite will not own that he is unrighteous, and the formalist will not confess that all his righteousnesses are as filthy rags. He thinks that his own righteousness is all that God requires of him, and that it will answer his purpose to the full. But the man with a broken heart and a contrite spirit will never be ashamed to say, in the presence of all men, "Yes, I was ragged, and lost, and ruined, and you have spoken a true word, though you meant it in ridicule; for I am nothing but a beggar wearing somebody else's garments." I like that trait in Christian's character, that the very thing with which these men twitted him, was that for which he felt that he had good reason to be grateful to God.

I am inclined to think, however, that Christian was not so wise in saying to these two men what he next told them. After speaking of his coat, he added:—

"'I have, moreover, a mark in my forehead, of which perhaps, you have taken no notice, which one of my Lord's most intimate associates fixed there in the day that my burden fell off my shoulders. I will tell you, moreover, that I had then given me a roll, sealed, to comfort me by reading, as I go on the way; I was also bid to give it in at the Celestial Gate, in token of my certain going in after it:

all which things, I doubt, you want, and want them because you came not in at the gate.'

"To these things they gave him no answer; only they looked upon each other, and laughed."

Of course they did; what did they know about the mark in the forehead and the roll in the hand? They had joined the church, they had "taken the sacrament," they had attended to the usual ceremonies; so they must all be right. "A mark in your forehead," said one, "what is the good of that?" "And the roll," said the other, "what is that?" Be not too fast, dear friends, in telling everybody about the secret of the Lord, or about your inward experience. When you meet with anyone who can appreciate these things, then make a point of glorifying God by your testimony; but when you are talking with a mere formalist, or a cunning hypocrite, it is better, as soon as you perceive that he is trusting to what he finds in himself, to show him the falsehood of his own supposed righteousness, than to say much concerning what the Lord has done for you. Beware of disobeying the command of our Lord concerning casting pearls before swine, lest they turn again, and rend you. When you talk of walking humbly with God, they will at once begin to laugh at you.

Bunyan's next description of the pilgrim always interests me; he says:—

"Then I saw that they went on all, save that Christian kept before, who had no more talk but with himself, and that sometimes sighingly and sometimes comfortably."

I know that John Bunyan never saw me, but he has sketched my portrait most accurately, for that is just the style in which I talk to myself, "sometimes sighingly and sometimes comfortably." I look within, and then I talk sighingly; then I look away to Christ, and that enables me to talk comfortably. I look around, and see all sorts of trials and troubles, and then I talk sighingly; then I look up to my Father's love, and I talk comfortably. I look sometimes to some of the Lord's people who are not walking as they should, and then I talk sighingly; then I think of the Lord's eternal purpose to present them faultless before the presence of His glory, and then I talk comfortably. A man passed me in the street, the other day, talking to himself so loudly that I thought he was speaking to me. It is not always wise to do that; but still, as we go through the world, we might talk to worse people than ourselves. May I make a suggestion, as I know some friends who are very fond of talking? If they would not mind talking more to themselves, the bad reputations of their neighbors would not be known quite so fast, and it would be quite as pleasant for themselves, I should think. Some people do love gossip and scandal; but it would be better if they would do as David did, and pour out their soul in talking to themselves. To talk about Divine things to your own soul, and to hold communion with your own heart upon your bed, is a wise and blessed exercise.

After that Bunyan goes on to say:—

"I beheld, then, that they all went on till they came to the foot of the Hill Difficulty; at the bottom of which was a spring. There were also in the same place two other ways besides that which came straight from the gate; one turned to the left hand, and the other to the right, at the bottom of the hill; but the narrow way lay right up the hill, and the name of the going up the side of the hill is called Difficulty."

Now comes the pinch. Christian has been through the Slough of Despond, so he is not afraid of climbing Hill Difficulty. He has been to the foot of the Cross, and there lost his burden, so he stoops down, and drinks at the spring, and says, "By God's help, I will climb the Hill Difficulty, too." Perhaps it was a little persecution, or maybe it was some discord in the church; perchance it was a loss in business, or it might have been some outward trial; but, whatever it was, he braced himself for the trial. The true Christian ever says within himself,—

"Through floods and flames, if Jesus lead,
  I'll follow where He goes."

But our friend Formalist saw that there was another
course open to him. He reasoned within himself that
it really was preposterous that people should be put
to any inconvenience for the sake of religion. We
often hear young people talk about what an ordeal they
have to go through, without knowing what an ordeal
really means; for, to go through an ordeal, was to walk
bare-footed over red-hot ploughshares. So Formalist
said that he did not mind being religious when it was
respectable, and if it involved no giving up of fashion-
able parties, or of marriage with an ungodly person;
but when it brought down the anger of a father, or the
opposition of one's old companions, he said he could
not endure that. So he would take the path that led
to the left, and wound round the bottom of the Hill
Difficulty; then he would come out on the other side,
where he should find Christian coming down with as
much difficulty as he went up, and then he would say
to him, "I have missed all this trouble, and yet have
come where you are, safe and sound." It was not so,
however, for Formalist went along the road called
Danger, which led him into a great wood, where he
was completely lost.

As for Hypocrisy, he took the road called Destruction, "which led him into a wide field, full of dark mountains, where he stumbled and fell, and rose no more." I suppose this means that he went off into the wilds of sin. He said to himself, "I have had enough of this kind of thing. If I am going to be abused for the sake of religion, or to lose my customers, I shall give it all up, and do as others do; I shall take my ease, and enjoy myself; I do not see why I should go on denying myself." So, beginning with one worldly pleasure, he went on to another and another, and soon, he "fell, and rose no more." The devil did not grow to be a devil in a day, and the worst of sinners do not become so all at once. A man may be a very decent-looking hypocrite for a long time. The horns and the hoofs may not peep out just yet; they grow by degrees, and show themselves in due time. The course of rebellion against God may be very gradual, but it increases in rapidity as you progress in it; and if you begin to run down the hill, the ever-increasing impetus will send you down faster and faster to destruction. You Christians ought to watch against the beginning of worldly conformity. I do believe that the growth of worldliness is like strife, which is as the letting out of water. Once you begin, there is no knowing where you will stop. I sometimes get this

question put to me, concerning certain worldly amuse-
ments, "May I do so-and-so?" I am very sorry whenever anyone asks me that question, because it shows
that there is something wrong, or it would not be raised
at all. If a person's conscience lets him say, "Well,
I can go to A," he will very soon go on to B, C, D, E,
and through all the letters of the alphabet. When
thieves would rob our houses, and find they cannot get
in at the front door, they search for a little window at
the back, and they put a small boy in there. As soon
as he is in, he opens the door to the thieves, and the
house is easily rifled. In so-called little sins there is
great mischief. When Satan cannot catch us with a
big sin, he will try a little one. It does not matter to
him, as long as he catches his fish, what bait he uses.
Beware of the beginning of evil, for many, who bade
fair to go right, have turned aside, and perished
amongst the dark mountains in the wide field of sin.

It is sad to have to speak thus concerning Formalist
and Hypocrisy, who were once as good people to look
upon as you and I now are, but who perished so miser-
ably. God grant that we may be neither formalists nor
hypocrites, but true pilgrims, to Zion's city bound,
and He shall have the praise and the glory!

IX.

CHRISTIAN ARRIVES AT THE PALACE BEAUTIFUL.

W E are now to consider John Bunyan's own description of Christian joining the church. He pictures one true pilgrim, namely, Faithful, who never did join the church, but went on his way alone until Christian overtook him. He was a great loser by doing so, as Christian said to him, when speaking of the Palace Beautiful, "I wish you had called at the house, for they would have showed you so many rarities, that you would scarce have forgot them to the day of your death." Still, Faithful, being an eminent saint, with great depth of knowledge, and experience, and with much firmness of conviction, served his Master well without joining the church; and you remember that Bunyan depicts him as being carried up, from the blazing fagots of martyrdom in Vanity Fair, in a chariot with a couple of horses, "through the clouds, with sound of trumpet, the nearest way to the Celestial Gate."

But Christian, and Christiana, and Mercy, and almost if not all the other pilgrims, stopped at the Palace Beautiful, by which Bunyan means the place of special Christian fellowship,—the Church of God on earth. This Palace Beautiful was a little beyond the top of the Hill Difficulty. Christian wasted some valuable time through sleeping in the arbour, losing his roll, and having to go back to find it; but, at last, says Bunyan,—

"while he was bewailing his unhappy miscarriage, he lift up his eyes, and, behold, there was a very stately palace before him, the name of which was Beautiful; and it stood just by the highway side.

"So I saw in my dream, that he made haste and went forward, that if possible he might get lodging there. Now before he had gone far, he entered into a very narrow passage, which was about a furlong off of the porter's lodge; and, looking very narrowly before him as he went, he espied two lions in the way."

When a person is about to be united with a Christian church, it often happens that he sees difficulties ahead, like these "two lions in the way." He begins to say to himself, "I cannot pass through such an ordeal." It seems to him such a trial to have to talk with a Christian brother about his experience, and a truly awful thing to have to come before the church, and a still more dreadful thing to be baptized; and, so, poor Mr. Timidity begins to quiver and quake. Sometimes, even worse fears than these come up, and the perplexed soul cries, "Shall I be able to hold on if I profess to be a follower of Christ? Shall I continue to bear a good testimony for Him in after years as well as now? What will my husband say about the matter? What will my father say? What will those I work with say when they hear that I have avowed myself to be a disciple of Christ? That was poor Christian's trouble "he espied two lions in the way."

" 'Now,' thought he, 'I see the dangers that Mistrust and Timorous were driven back by.' (The lions were chained but he saw not the chains.)"

Unbelief generally has a good eye for the lions, but a blind eye for the chains that hold them back. It is quite true that there are difficulties in the way of those who profess to be followers of the Lord Jesus Christ. We do not desire to conceal this fact, and we do not wish you to come amongst us without counting the cost. But it is also true that these difficulties have a limit which they cannot pass. Like the lions in the pilgrim's pathway, they are chained, and restrained, and absolutely under the control of the Lord God Almighty.

"Then he was afraid, and thought nothing but death was before him. But the porter at the lodge, whose name is Watchful, perceiving that Christian made a halt as if he would go back, cried unto him, saying, 'Is thy strength so small? (Mark xiii. 34-37.) Fear not the lions, for they are chained, and are placed there for trial of faith where it is, and for discovery of those that have none. Keep in the midst of the path, and no hurt shall come unto thee.'"

Watchful means the good minister, who ought to be ever watchful for souls. He told the pilgrim to "keep in the midst of the path;" and we give you the same advice. Live consistently, walk carefully;— not right at the edge of the way, as though you were half inclined to wander from it; but on the crown of the causeway, right in the middle of the King's highway. Walk in integrity and uprightness, whatever may be the consequence of doing so. For a while, difficulties may dismay you, but they really cannot hurt you. The lions are chained.

What is the difficulty in the way of any of you who desire to make a profession of your faith in Christ? I ask you earnestly to look it in the face; for, I believe, if you do so, it will soon vanish. Consider the difficulty carefully, and then consider the far greater difficulty in your way if you do *not* profess the faith which you say that you do truly hold. Remember these words of the Lord Jesus, which you can never explain away, "He that denieth Me before men shall be denied before the angels of God." "Oh!" you say, "I do not deny Christ; I merely do not confess Him." Yes, but that is just what our Saviour meant by denial of Him, for He had just before said, "Whosoever shall confess Me before men, him shall the Son of man also confess before the angels of God;" so that the expression, "He that denieth Me before men" is evidently intended to apply to him who does not confess Christ. Therefore, see to it that you do come forward, and testify that you belong to Christ, if you really are His. When Israel turned aside to worship the golden calf, "Moses stood in the gate of the camp, and said, Who is on the Lord's side? let him come unto me. And all the sons of Levi gathered themselves together unto him." May there be many such who will now come, and avow their faith, because the Lord has by His grace, called them unto Himself!

"Then I saw that he went on, trembling for fear of the lions; but taking good heed to the directions of the porter; he heard them roar, but they did him no harm. Then he clapped his hands, and went on till he came and stood before the gate where the porter was. Then said Christian, to the porter, 'Sir, what house is this? And may I lodge here to-night?' The porter answered, 'This house was built by the Lord of the hill, and He built it for the relief and security of pilgrims.'"

The purpose for which the Palace Beautiful—the Church of the living God—was established, is that "pilgrims to Zion's city bound" may there find rest, refreshment, shelter, and protection. I wonder what

some of us would have done if it had not been for the
Sabbath services of the sanctuary, the gathering of
ourselves together for worship in its varied forms of
preaching, prayer, and praise. When I am away from
England, travelling on the Continent,—in places where
there is no public assembly for worship,—as the Sabbaths come round, I always try to meet with two or
three Christian friends, that we may read the Word
of God together, and pray, and sing, and, if possible,
remember our Lord in the breaking of bread; and we
have found Christ very precious at such times. Yet,
for all that, I always miss this Tabernacle, and its
hallowed services; nothing can fill their place in my
heart. I have often felt just as the psalmist did when
he was away from Jerusalem; it seemed almost more
than he could bear, and he longed to enjoy even the
meanest place within the Courts of the Lord's house.
I feel sure that it must be so with all of you who love
the Lord; if you were banished from the place where
God's name is specially recorded, and where you have
so often been fed with the finest of the wheat, what
would you do? Perhaps it is night with some of you,
as it was with Christian when he came to the Palace
Beautiful; and, therefore, you want shelter, and much
beside. Well, the Church of Christ is ordained for this
very purpose,—that, by the use of the means of grace,

and by mutual fellowship, Christians may be comforted and relieved.

"The porter also asked whence he was, and whither he was going.

"CHR. I am come from the City of Destruction, and am going to Mount Zion; but because the sun is now set, I desire, if I may, to lodge here to-night.

"POR. What is your name?

"CHR. My name is now Christian, but my name at the first was Graceless; I came of the race of Japheth, whom God will persuade to dwell in the tents of Shem. (Genesis ix. 27.)

"POR. But how doth it happen you come so late? The sun is set."

Ah! that is a question I often have to ask pilgrims,— "Why have you come so late to join the church? Why did you not confess Christ sooner?" So many put off this very important matter for a long while, as though it were of no account. I notice that, if they postpone it for a month or two, they are very apt to put it off for a year or two; and if they do that, they are most likely to put it off for a still longer period. They have been truly converted, they are believers in the Lord Jesus Christ, and yet, because they do not join the church at the first, they have continued postponing and postponing until some of them have actually died out of membership with the church. I do not say, of course, that they have been lost through this neglect; but I do say that they have lost many blessings, and many opportunities of glorifying God by the way, through their disobedience to His plain command.

Christian had to make a very sorrowful confession :—

> " 'I had been here sooner, but that, "wretched man that I am!" I slept in the arbour that stands on the hill-side; nay, I had, notwithstanding that, been here much sooner, but that, in my sleep, I lost my evidence, and came without it to the brow of the hill, and then, feeling for it, and finding it not, I was forced, with sorrow of heart, to go back to the place where I slept my sleep, where I found it: and now I am come.' "

He gave the true reason for arriving so late at the Palace Beautiful, but it was a great pity that he had to admit that he had been slumbering, and so had lost his evidence, and was obliged to go back for it. When you and I fall into a sleepy state, we are very liable to lose our evidences, and to think that we are not children of God at all. In this way, we lose our first love, our highest joys, and the unwavering confidence in God that we once possessed; and we rightly feel, that we cannot join the church till we get these blessings back; so, like poor Christian, we have to go down Hill Difficulty, and to toil up the steep ascent again,— treading the same road three times instead of only once, just because we went to sleep in the arbour when we ought to have been pressing on towards the Palace Beautiful. Thrice happy shall we be if, like the pilgrim, though late, we safely reach the gate of that holy house "built by the Lord of the hill for the relief and security of pilgrims."

WATCHFUL INTRODUCES CHRISTIAN TO DISCRETION

"This man is on a journey from the City of Destruction
to Mount Zion."

X

"COME IN, THOU BLESSED OF THE LORD."

"The porter then said to Christian, 'Well, I will call out one of the virgins of this place, who will, if she likes your talk, bring you in to the rest of the family, according to the rules of the house.' "

JOHN BUNYAN was a member of a Baptist church, and he knew how to do things in an orderly manner. I have sometimes met with people who have said that, in reading "The Pilgrim's Progress," you cannot tell to what denomination the writer belonged; but if you study his book carefully, you will soon discover, both from what he left out and what he put in, what the good man's position was. When John Bunyan joined Mr. Gifford's church, the Pastor said to him, "Well, John, I am glad to find that you are converted, but I could not take upon myself the responsibility of receiving you into fellowship; I must ask one of my elders or deacons to see you. Someone must be appointed by the church to converse with you, and to report to the rest of the members whether you should be received or not."

"So Watchful, the porter, rang a bell, at the sound of which came out at the door of the house, a grave and beautiful damsel, named Discretion, and asked why she was called."

The officer of the church, who is appointed to see candidates for membership, should be "grave" in his carriage and "beautiful" in his character; he should be discreet, yet affectionate; desirous neither to be deceived nor to let his fellow-members be deceived; anxious not to be too severe, so as to keep out of the church those who are truly the Lord's; and, on the other hand, not to be too lax, so as to receive those who are not His people.

"The porter answered, 'This man is in a journey from the City of Destruction to Mount Zion, but being weary and benighted, he asked me if he might lodge here to-night; so I told him I would call for thee, who, after discourse had with him, mayest do as seemeth thee good, even according to the law of the house.' Then she asked him whence he was, and whither he was going; and he told her."

This is like the examination of converts which we generally describe under the term "seeing the elders." In answer to the enquiries of Discretion, Christian did not go beating about the bush, and talking of other matters, but he told her at once what she wanted to know. "She asked him whence he was." That question was put in order to ascertain whether he knew what he was by nature; for, if you do not know what you are by nature, you do not really begin to know anything aright. If you have never discovered that you were born in sin, and shapen in iniquity,—if you

have never realized that you are a sinner, lost and undone;—and, further, if you have never lost your burden at the cross,—you are not fit to be entertained
at the Palace Beautiful, for you evidently are not a
true Christian.

Next, Discretion asked Christian "whither he was
going." That is a very important question. I am
afraid that there are many people who do not know
whither they are going,—whether to Heaven or to
hell,—though they have a faint hope that, possibly, all
may be well with them at the last. There are also
some who assert that a man cannot know whether he
is saved till he gets into another world. Surely, they
must have read a different Bible from the one I read
every day; for that seems to me to speak very clearly
upon this matter: "He that believeth and is baptized
shall be saved;"—"Therefore being justified by faith,
we have peace with God through our Lord Jesus
Christ." Surely, a man is not saved without knowing
it; and he does not possess peace with God without
being aware that he has that peace.

"She asked him also how he had got into the way; and
he told her."

That is another enquiry that we shall put to you if
you wish to unite with us in church-fellowship. We
shall say to you, "You profess to be on the road to

Heaven; but how did you commence to walk in that way? What led you to go on pilgrimage? How came you to realize your need of a Saviour? How did the work of grace begin in your heart? We shall not want you to tell us the day and the hour when you were converted. Some of us could tell that about ourselves, but others could not; and there will be no discreet virgin who will be angry with you if you cannot. Often, when it rains, it would puzzle a Solomon to tell you exactly when it began, for it was at first a kind of mist, then it turned to a little drizzle, and afterwards it did really rain. When you were wet through, you knew that it had been raining; yet you could not have told when it began. Oftentimes, when the sun is shining, it may be that nobody can tell just when it rose, yet you know that it did rise, for you can both see it and feel it. When I was in Switzerland, one afternoon, I went up some five thousand feet so as to sleep at an inn, and to be ready for the sunrise the following day. Early in the morning, a big horn was blown, and everybody jumped out of bed, for that was an intimation that the sun was rising. We all ran out, wrapped in our blankets,—perhaps two hundred of us,—and were all staring away at the East to see the sun rise; but we were too late, for the sun was up before we were there. So is it, often, with the work of grace in the heart. It is there, but you do not know when it came there. This is one point upon which the discreet virgin will be sure to question you, and I trust that we shall be able to say of you, as Bunyan says of Christian, "and he told her."

"Then she asked him what he had seen and met with in the way; and he told her."

We shall want to know what your experience has been since you became a Christian,—whether you have proved the power of the prayer, because God has answered your petitions,—whether, when you have been tempted, you have been able to resist the tempter, and overcome him. We shall also ask you what you are doing for Christ, and what you think of Christ, and what are your habits with regard to reading the Scriptures, and private prayer, and such things.

"And last she asked his name; so he said, 'It is Christian, and I have so much the more a desire to lodge here to-night, because, by what I perceive, this place was built by the Lord of the hill, for the relief and security of pilgrims.' So she smiled, but the water stood in her eyes; and after a little pause, she said, 'I will call forth two or three more of the family.' "

You see, she was a tender, affectionate, gentle creature. She smiled to hear what the pilgrim said; she was pleased with his testimony, and "the water stood in her eyes" as she blessed the Lord that there was another soul brought out of darkness into His marvellous light.

You have, in this passage, a reference to the different church-officers. Mr. Watchful was the minister; Discretion was the deacon or elder; and then came "two or three more of the family."

"So she ran to the door, and called out Prudence, Piety, and Charity."

These are the messengers of the church :—Prudence, who does not want to let any hypocrites in; Piety, who understands spiritual matters, and knows how to search the heart; and Charity, who judges kindly, yet justly, according to the love of Christ which is shed abroad in her heart.

"Prudence, Piety, and Charity, after a little more discourse with him, had him into the family; and many of them, meeting him at the threshold of the house, said, 'Come in, thou blessed of the Lord;' this house was built by the Lord of the hill, on purpose to entertain such pilgrims in. Then he bowed his head, and followed them into the house. So when he was come in and sat down, they gave him something to drink, and consented together that, until supper was ready, some of them should have some particular discourse with Christian, for the best improvement of time; and they appointed Piety, and Prudence, and Charity to discourse with him."

There I shall leave him for the present, in good snug quarters, and I hope many of you will be tempted to come to the same door, and by the same means enter into the quietude and security of the Palace Beautiful, —Christ's Church on earth.

CHRISTIAN GIVES THANKS FOR
VICTORY

XI.

CHRISTIAN AND APOLLYON.

"Now Christian bethought himself of setting forward, and they were willing he should. 'But first,' said they, 'let us go again into the armoury.' So they did, and when he came there, they harnessed him from head to foot with what was of proof, lest perhaps he should meet with assaults in the way."

JOHN BUNYAN, with great wisdom, puts the Palace Beautiful first, and then no sooner does Christian get out of the Palace gates than he begins to descend into the Valley of Humiliation. They had given him a sword, and a shield, and a helmet. He had never had those before. Now that he had his sword, he found that he had to use it against Apollyon; now that he had his shield, he had to hold it up to catch the fiery dart; now that he had received the weapon of "All prayer," he found that he had need of it as he walked through that desperate place, the Valley of the Shadow of Death. God does not give His people weapons to play with; He does not give them strength to spend on their lusts. Lord, if Thou hast given me these goodly weapons, it is sure I shall need them in hard fighting. If I have had a feast at Thy table, I will remember that it is but a short walk from the upper chamber to the garden of Gethsemane. Daniel, the man greatly beloved, was reduced very low. "All his comeliness was turned into corruption and he retained no strength," when God shewed him "the great vision." Thus, too, with favoured John. He must be banished to Patmos; in the deep solitude of that Ægean sea-girt island he must receive "the Revelation of Jesus Christ which God gave unto him." I have noticed, in the ordinary scenes of Christian experience, that our greatest joys come just after some of our sorest trials. When the howling tempest has played out its strength, it soothes itself to sleep. Then comes a season of calm and quiet, so profound in its stillness, that only the monstrous tempest could have been the mother of so mighty a calm. So seems it with us. Deep waves of trial, high mountains of joy. But the reverse is almost as often true; from Pisgah's top we pass to our graves; from the top of Carmel we have to go down to the dens of lions, and to fight with the leopards. Let us be on our watch-tower, lest like Manoah, having seen the angel of God, the next thing should be that we say we shall surely die, for we have seen the Lord.

"Then he began to go forward; but Discretion, Piety, Charity, and Prudence would accompany him down to the foot of the hill. So they went on together reiterating their former discourses, till they came to go down the hill. Then said Christian, 'As it was difficult coming up, so, so far as I can see, it is dangerous going down.' 'Yes,' said Prudence, 'so it is: for it is a hard matter for a man to go down into the Valley of Humiliation, as thou art now, and to catch no slip by the way;' 'therefore,' said they, 'are we come out to accompany thee down the hill.' So he began to go down, but very warily: yet he caught a slip or two."

Satan does not often attack a Christian who is living near to God. It is when the Christian departs from his God, becomes spiritually starved, and endeavours to feed on vanities, that the devil discovers his vantage hour. He may sometimes stand foot to foot with the child of God who is active in his Master's service, but the battle is generally short. He who slips as he goes down into the Valley of Humiliation, every time he takes a false step invites Apollyon to assail him. Oh, for grace to walk humbly with our God!

"Then I saw in my dream, that these good companions, when Christian was gone down to the bottom of the hill, gave him a loaf of bread, a bottle of wine, and a cluster of raisins, and then he went his way.

"But now, in this Valley of Humiliation, poor Christian was hard put to it; for he had gone but a little way before he espied a foul fiend coming over the field to meet him: his name is Apollyon. Then did Christian begin to be afraid, and to cast in his mind whether to go back, or to stand his ground. But he considered again that he had no armour for his back, and therefore thought that to turn

the back to him might give him greater advantage with ease
to pierce him with his darts; therefore he resolved to venture,
and stand his ground; 'for,' thought he, 'had I no more in
mine eye than the saving of my life, it would be the best
way to stand.' '

John Bunyan has not pictured Christian as carried
to heaven while asleep in an easy chair. He makes
him lose his burden at the cross-foot, but he represents
him as climbing Hill Difficulty on his hands and knees.
Christian has to descend into the Valley of Humiliation, and to tread the dangerous pathway through the
gloomy horrors of the Shadow of Death. He has to
be urgently watchful to keep himself from sleeping in
the Enchanted Ground. Nowhere is he delivered from
the necessities incident to the way, for even at the last
he fords the black river, and struggles with its terrible
billows. Effort is used all the way through, and you
that are pilgrims to the skies will find it to be no allegory, but a real matter of fact. Your soul must gird
up her loins; you need your pilgrim's staff, and your
armour. You must foot it all the way to heaven, contending with giants, fighting with lions, and combat-
ing Apollyon himself.

"So he went on, and Apollyon met him. Now the mon-
ster was hideous to behold; he was clothed with scales
like a fish, and they are his pride; he had wings like a
dragon, and feet like a bear, and out of his belly came fire

and smoke; and his mouth was as the mouth of a lion. When he was come up to Christian, he beheld him with a disdainful countenance, and thus began to question with him.

"APOLLYON. Whence came you, and whither are you bound?

"CHR. I am come from the City of Destruction, which is the place of all evil, and I am going to the City of Zion.

"APOL. By this I perceive that thou art one of my subjects; for all that country is mine, and I am the prince and god of it. How is it, then, that thou hast run away from thy king? Were it not that I hope that thou mayest do me more service, I would strike thee now at one blow to the ground.

"CHR. I was indeed born in your dominions, but your service was hard, and your wages such as a man could not live on; for the wages of sin is death (Rom. vi. 23); therefore when I was come to years, I did, as other considerate persons do, look out, if perhaps I might mend myself.

"APOL. There is no prince that will thus lightly lose his subjects, neither will I as yet lose thee; but since thou complainest of thy service and wages, be content to go back, and what our country will afford, I do here promise to give thee.

"CHR. But I have let myself to another, even to the King of princes; and how can I with fairness go back with thee?

"APOL. Thou hast done in this according to the proverb, 'changed a bad for worse;' but it is ordinary for those that have professed themselves His servants, after a while to give Him the slip, and return again to me. Do thou so too, and all shall be well.

"CHR. I have given Him my faith, and sworn my allegiance to Him; how then can I go back from this, and not be hanged as a traitor?

"APOL. Thou didst the same to me, and yet I am willing to pass by all, if now thou wilt yet turn again and go back.

"CHR. What I promised thee was in my nonage; and besides, I count that the Prince, under whose banner I now stand, is able to absolve me, yea, and to pardon also what I did as to my compliance with thee. And besides, O thou destroying Apollyon, to speak truth, I like His service, His wages, His servants, His government, His company, and country, better than thine; therefore leave off to persuade me further; I am His servant, and I will follow Him."

I have met with some who were of a fearful heart, afraid that they would be lost, *because they felt that they had, at some period of their lives, neglected Christian duty.* This is an old temptation that Satan often casts in the way of godly people. You remember how, in addition to the base insinuations which we have quoted, Apollyon charged poor Christian with being unfaithful:

"Thou didst faint at first setting out, when thou wast almost choked in the Gulf of Despond; thou didst attempt wrong ways to be rid of thy burden, whereas thou shouldest have stayed till thy Prince had taken it off; thou didst sinfully sleep, and lose thy choice thing; thou wast, also, almost persuaded to go back, at the sight of the lions; and when thou talkest of thy journey, and of what thou hast heard and seen, thou art inwardly desirous of vain-glory in all that thou sayest or doest."

Now, if any of you should be troubled by similar accusations of the adversary, recollect that, since Christ did not love you for your good works,—they were not the cause of His beginning to love you;—so He does not love you for your good works even now; they are not the cause of His continuing to love you. He loves you because He will love you. What He approves in you now is that which He has Himself given to you; that is always the same, it ever abideth as it was. The life of God is ever within you; Jesus has not turned away His heart from you, nor has the flame of His love decreased in the smallest degree. Wherefore, faint heart, "fear not, be strong."

"APOL. Then Apollyon broke out into a grievous rage, saying, I am an enemy to this Prince; I hate His person, His laws, and people; I am come out on purpose to withstand thee.

"CHR. Apollyon, beware what you do, for I am in the King's highway, the way of Holiness; therefore take heed to yourself.

"APOL. Then Apollyon straddled quite over the whole breadth of the way, and said, I am void of fear in this matter. Prepare thyself to die; for I swear by my infernal den, that thou shalt go no farther: here will I spill thy soul. And with that he threw a flaming dart at his breast; but Christian had a shield in his hand, with which he caught it, and so prevented the danger of that.

"Then did Christian draw, for he saw it was time to bestir him; and Apollyon as fast made at him, throwing darts as thick as hail; by the which, notwithstanding all that Christian could do to avoid it, Apollyon wounded him in his head, his hand and foot. This made Christian give a little back; Apollyon, therefore, followed his work amain, and Christian again took courage, and resisted as manfully as he could. This sore combat lasted for above half a day, even till Christian was almost quite spent. For you must know, that Christian, by reason of his wounds, must needs grow weaker and weaker."

This is no mere figure. He that hath ever met Apollyon will tell you that there is no mistake about the matter, but that there is a dread reality in it. Christian met Apollyon when he was in the Valley of Humiliation, and the dragon did most fiercely beset him; with fiery darts he sought to destroy him and to take away his life. Brave Christian stood to him with all his might, and used his sword and shield right manfully, till his shield became studded with a forest of darts and his hand did cleave unto his sword. For many an hour man and dragon fought. I think I see him now before me,—that dread fallen spirit, the arch-enemy of our souls. "O Satan, thou hast thrust sore at me!" Many a child of God must utter this exclamation. It is no fault of Satan's if we are not quite destroyed. It is not for want of malice, or subtlety, or fury, or perseverance on the devil's part, if we still hold the field. He has met us many times, using all kinds of weapons, shooting from the right hand and from the left. He has tempted us to pride and despair, to care and to carelessness, to presumption and to idleness, to self-confidence and to mistrust of God. We are not ignorant of his devices, nor inexperienced in his cruelties.

I know that I am addressing many saints of God who can use David's language with emphasis: "Thou hast thrust sore at me that I might fall," for I dwell among a tried and tempted people. The battle between the soul of the believer and the devil is a stern one. No doubt there are multitudes of inferior spirits who tempt men, and tempt them successfully, too; but they are much more easily put aside by godly men than their great leader can be.

"Then Apollyon, espying his opportunity, began to gather up close to Christian, and wrestling with him, gave him a dreadful fall; and with that Christian's sword flew out of his hand. Then said Apollyon, 'I am sure of thee now.' And with that he had almost pressed him to death; so that Christian began to despair of life. But as God would have it, while Apollyon was fetching his last blow, thereby to make a full end of this good man, Christian nimbly reached out his hand for his sword, and caught it, saying, 'Rejoice not against me, O mine enemy; when I fall, I shall arise;' and with that gave him a deadly thrust, which made him give back, as one that had received his mortal wound. Christian, perceiving that, made at him again, saying, 'Nay, in all these things we are more than conquerors through Him that loved us' (Rom. viii. 37). And with that Apollyon spread forth his dragon's wings, and sped him away, that Christian saw him no more (James iv. 7)."

At last the fiend gave Christian a horrible fall, and down he went upon the ground; and, woe worth the day! at the moment when he fell he dropped his sword! Behold the dragon drawing up all his might, planting his foot upon Christian's neck, and about to hurl the fiery dart into his heart. "Aha, I have thee now," saith he, "thou art in my power." But when the dragon's foot was about to crush the very life out of poor Christian, he did stretch out his hand, he grasped his sword and giving a desperate thrust at his foe, he cried, "Rejoice not over me, O mine enemy; for when I fall I shall arise again." So desperately did he cut the dragon, that he spread his wings and flew away, and Christian went on his journey rejoicing in his victory.

The true believer understands all this. It is no dream to him. He has been under the dragon's foot many a time. Ah! and all the world put on a man's heart at once is not equal in weight to one foot of the devil. When Satan once gets the upper hand of the spirit, he wants neither strength, nor will, nor malice, to torment it. Hard is that man's lot who has fallen beneath the hoof of the Evil One. But, blessed be God, the child of God is ever safe, as safe beneath the dragon's foot as he shall be before the throne of God in heaven. And let all the powers of earth and hell and all the doubts and fears that Christians ever know, conspire together to molest a saint; in the darkest moment, lo, God shall arise, and His enemies shall be scattered, and He shall get unto Himself the victory. Oh, for faith to believe this!

"In this combat no man can imagine, unless he had seen and heard as I did, what yelling and hideous roaring Apollyon made all the time of the fight; he spake like a dragon; and, on the other side, what sighs and groans burst from Christian's heart. I never saw him all the while give so much as one pleasant look, till he perceived he had wounded Apollyon with his two-edged sword; then, indeed, he did smile, and look upwards; but it was the dreadfullest fight that I ever saw."

Apollyon is master of legions, and possesses the highest degree of power and craftiness. He who has once stood foot to foot with him will know that Christian was indeed hard put to it in the Valley of Humiliation, when the dragon stopped the pilgrim's way, and made him fight for his life.

No Christian will find much to smile at while he is contending for his faith, his hope, his life, with this most cruel of foes. Messengers of Satan buffet us terribly, but Satan himself wounds desperately; wherefore we are wisely taught to pray, "Deliver us from the evil one." Single combat with the arch-enemy will strain every muscle of the soul, and pain every nerve of the spirit; it will force the cold sweat from the brow, and make the heart leap with palpitations of fear, and thus in some degree bring us to our Gethsemane, and make us feel that the pains of hell have gotten hold upon us. This prince of darkness has a sharp sword, great cunning of fence, tremendous power of aim, and boundless malice of heart, and thus he is no mean adversary, but one whom it is a terrible trial to meet. In his dread personality is contained a mass of danger for us poor mortals. When poor Christian was down under Apollyon's foot, his life was nearly pressed out of him; but he saw that, as God would have it, the sword which had fallen out of his hand was just within his reach, so he stretched out his hand, and grasped that "sword of the Spirit, which is the Word of God," and therewith he gave his adversary such a terrible stab that he spread his dragon-wings, and flew away Oh, to give the fiend such a stab as that! Let us tell out the promises; let us proclaim the gospel; let us publish · everywhere the free grace of God; and in this way we shall turn the battle to the gate, and cause those who pursued us to be themselves pursued. Hallelujah for the cross of Christ! We bear it forward into the ranks of the foe, confident of victory. Our courage fails not, neither does our hope wax faint; the Lord who has helped us is the God of victories; "the Lord of Hosts is with us, the God of Jacob is our refuge."

HOPEFUL JOINS CHRISTIAN

"There was one whose name was Hopeful who joined himself
unto him."

XII.

WHAT FAITHFUL MET WITH IN THE WAY.

"CHRISTIAN. Well, neighbour Faithful, tell me now, what have you met with in the way as you came; for I know you have met with some things, or else it may be writ for a wonder.

"FAITHFUL. I escaped the Slough that I perceived you fell into, and got up to the gate without that danger; only I met with one whose name was Wanton, who had like to have done me a mischief.

"CHR. It was well you escaped her net; Joseph was hard put to it by her, and he escaped her as you did; but it had like to have cost him his life. But what did she do to you?

"FAITH. You cannot think, but that you know something, what a flattering tongue she had; she lay at me hard to turn aside with her, promising me all manner of content.

"CHR. Nay, she did not promise you the content of a good conscience.

"FAITH. You know what I mean; all carnal and fleshly content.

"CHR. Thank God you have escaped her: 'The abhorred of the Lord shall fall into her ditch.' (Prov. xxii. 14.)

"FAITH. Nay, I know not whether I did wholly escape her or no.

"CHR. Why, I trow you did not consent to her desires.

"FAITH. No, not to defile myself; for I remembered an old writing that I had seen, which said, 'Her steps take hold on hell.' (Prov. v. 5.) So I shut mine eyes, because I would not be bewitched with her looks. (Job xxxi. 1.) Then she railed on me, and I went my way."

145

THE first of Faithful's temptations was very gross. It is, indeed, almost a shame to speak of it; yet the purest and most heavenly-minded, being still in the body, have to confess that this temptation has crossed their path. It matters not how near we live to God, nor how we may have cleansed our way by taking heed thereto according to God's Word, to us all, and I have sometimes thought especially to the young and to the aged, this temptation will surely come. It is a blessing if, by God's grace, we use Joseph's way of conquering it, namely, by running away from it, for there is no other. Fly, for this foe is not to be parleyed with. While you tarry, you are taken prisoner. While you look, the fruit is plucked. While you think how to resist the attack of the serpent, you are caught in its folds. He that hesitates is lost. "Escape for thy life, look not behind thee, neither stay thou in all the plain," is the only direction to every man who would come out of Sodom. There is no way of escape from this sin save by flight. "Flee youthful lusts," wrote Paul to Timothy.

Observe that, although Faithful did not yield to Wanton's tempting, he says, "I know not whether I did wholly escape her or no." The probability is, that the temptations of the flesh, even when resisted, do us an injury. If the coals do not burn us, they blacken us. The very thought of evil, and especially of such evil, is sin. We can hardly read a newspaper report of anything of this kind without having our minds in some degree defiled. There are certain flowers which perfume the air as they bloom, and I may say of these matters that they scatter an ill savour as they are repeated in our ears. So much for Wanton's assault on Faithful. From her net, and her ditch, may every pilgrim be preserved!

"Chr. Did you meet with no other assault as you came?

"Faith. When I came to the foot of the hill called Difficulty, I met with a very aged man, who asked me what I was, and whither bound. I told him that I was a pilgrim, going to the Celestial City. Then said the old man, 'Thou lookest like an honest fellow; wilt thou be content to dwell with me for the wages that I shall give thee?' Then I asked him his name and where he dwelt. He said his name was Adam the First, and that he dwelt in the town of Deceit. (Eph. iv. 22.) I asked him then what was his work, and what the wages that he would give. He told me, that his work was many delights; and his wages, that I should be his heir at last. I further asked him, what house he kept, and what other servants he had. So he told me, that his house was maintained with all the dainties in the world; and that his servants were those of his own begetting. Then I asked him if he had any children. He said he had but three daughters; the Lust of the Flesh, the Lust of the Eyes, and the Pride of Life, and that I should marry them all if I would. (1 John ii. 16.) Then I asked, how long time he would have me live with him? And he told me, as long as he lived himself."

I suppose that every Christian, who has gone far on the road to Heaven, knows what Faithful means when he speaks of Adam the First. Still, it may be well to contemplate it for a little, for so we shall be constrained to praise the mighty grace which delivers us from the power of this father of all mischief,—the old Adam-nature that is in us.

First, observe that this nature is described as an old man. Some of you, perhaps, have not been converted more than two or three years, but you are thirty years old, so the old nature is thirty, though the new nature is only three. Some, who are seventy years of age, may yet be only babes in grace. How can we expect the babe, that is newly born, to be a match for the old man, unless God shall come to the rescue, and give superior strength?

This old man met the pilgrim, and called him "an honest fellow." Just so; our old nature would always have us think well of ourselves. God's Word says that "the heart is deceitful above all things." Among other deceits that it practices, it always seeks to flatter us. Oh, yes, we are indeed wonderfully honest fellows! I have known men, who have committed all sorts of sins, who have prided themselves upon being surprisingly honest. They are no hypocrites! They make no pretence of being religious. They hate cant, and so on, and so on. Beware of the compliment your own heart pays you.

Then Old Adam asked Faithful to go home with him. Observe, he promised him wages. Under the Old Adam, it is all wage; under the New Adam, it is not of debt, but of grace. The old gentleman told him what the wages would be. He said that Faithful should be his heir at the last. A pretty inheritance that would be, for "the wages of sin is death;" and if we walk after the flesh, we shall of the flesh reap corruption. We shall only inherit what the Old Adam leaves us, and what does that mean but that we shall be heirs of wrath, even as others? A poor look-out for a servant to engage where eternal wrath must be the wages of his service!

As for the work, Old Adam said it would be all manner of delights. Yes, there is pleasure in sin, of a sort. The carnal mind will appreciate it. The froth on the top of the cup gleams with so many rainbow colours, and the taste thereof is so sweet at first, that he who drinks forgets what the dregs are, which God says all the wicked of the earth shall wring out. Even in this life he must drink of them, and in the life to come he must experience eternal destruction from the presence of the Lord. Then the old man said that his house was maintained with all the dainties in the world; and that is true, for the old nature seeks after all things to delight itself, and yet is never contented. When Solomon became its votary, he took to himself servants and maidens, men singers and women singers, music, and wine, and all manner of delights, and yet he had to say, "Vanity of vanities; all is vanity." All the delights of the flesh are nothing better than a delusion. How soon they are over and gone! The blaze of a few thorns is quickly past, and a handful of ashes is all that remains.

As for the three daughters of the old man, you know them. Of the Lust of the Flesh, we have already spoken under the head of wantonness. Then there is the Lust of the Eyes. The eye can scarcely look upon a thing of beauty without desiring it. We soon become covetous unless the Spirit of God keeps our mind under proper restraint. "Thou shalt not covet," is a commandment which is often broken by us almost unconsciously. Consequently, we do not repent as we should of our sin against that commandment which touches our thoughts and our desires. As to the Pride of Life, I am afraid that many Christians truckle to this third daughter of the First Adam by self-indulgence in dress, in expenses, in all sorts of showiness.

Mark you, this Pride of Life, though the most respectable of the three, as people think, is as genuine a daughter of the Old Adam as is the Lust of the Flesh. I cannot imagine our Lord Jesus Christ dressing Himself so as to attract attention to His person; neither can I imagine Mary Magdalene, or Mary and Martha, the sisters of Lazarus, caring for mere show and pomp. I cannot picture them walking so in the light of their Master's countenance. They were arrayed, rather, like those holy women in the old time, whose adorning was not that of plaited hair and gorgeous apparel, but of all the ornaments of a meek and quiet spirit. This daughter of the Old Adam is much set by in these days. She keeps the milliners' shops going, and she sends many a man into the bankruptcy court; and, alas! she is invited into many of our Christian circles, and thought right well of.

Old Adam proposed that Faithful should marry all these if he would. There are some who have entered into this dreadful triple wedlock, and they have had a terrible threefold curse as the result.

Notice how long the service was to be. He told Faithful that he would have him live with him "as long as he lived himself." When a man gives himself up to the Old Adam, he never gets free from the service, for, while the Old Adam has his snares for the young, he has also his temptations for the middle-aged, and I am certain that he has quite as many for the old. This serpent can suit himself to every age and disposition, nor is there a hole so small but he can wriggle into it. The service of sin is a life-long service, and the end of it is everlasting woe.

"CHR. Well, and what conclusion came the old man and you to, at last?

"FAITH. Why, at first, I found myself somewhat inclinable to go with the man, for I thought he spake very fair; but looking in his forehead, as I talked with him, I saw there written, 'Put off the old man with his deeds.'"

What a mercy it was that Faithful was led to inspect the old man! We only need to look at him to see what he is. He is so transparently bad that, if a man will but put his "considering-cap" on, he must soon see that "the old man" is to be "put off, with his deeds." Conscience, I think, is sufficiently alert in all of us to tell us that self-indulgence, in any of its forms, cannot be right for the followers of the holy Jesus. "Put off the old man with his deeds," was the brand across his brow; and as soon as Faithful saw that, he declined to have anything more to do with him.

XIII.

WHAT FAITHFUL MET WITH IN THE WAY.
(Conclusion.)

"CHR. And how then?

"FAITH. Then it came burning hot into my mind, whatever he said, and however he flattered, when he got me home to his house, he would sell me for a slave. So I bid him forbear to talk, for I would not come near the door of his house. Then he reviled me, and told me, that he would send such a one after me, that should make my way bitter to my soul. So I turned to go away from him; but just as I turned myself to go thence, I felt him take hold of my flesh, and give me such a deadly twitch back, that I thought he had pulled part of me after himself. This made me cry, 'O wretched man!' (Rom. vii. 24.) So I went on my way up the hill. Now when I had got about half-way up, I looked behind, and saw one coming after me, swift as the wind; so he overtook me just about the place where the settle stands. So soon as the man overtook me, he was but a word and a blow, for down he knocked me, and laid me for dead. But when I was a little come to myself again, I asked him wherefore he served me so. He said, because of my secret inclining to Adam the First: and with that he struck me another deadly blow on the breast, and beat me down backward; so I lay at his foot as dead as before. So, when I came to myself again, I cried him mercy; but he said, 'I know not how to show mercy;' and with that knocked me down again. He had doubtless made an end of me, but that One came by, and bid him forbear.

"CHR. Who was that that bid him forbear?

"Faith. I did not know Him at first, but as He went by, I perceived the holes in His hands, and in His side; then I concluded that He was our Lord. So I went up the hill.

"Chr. That man that overtook you was Moses. He spareth none, neither knoweth he how to show mercy to those that transgress his law.

"Faith. I know it very well; it was not the first time that he has met with me. It was he that came to me when I dwelt securely at home, and that told me he would burn my house over my head if I stayed there."

FAITHFUL said, "Then it came burning hot into my mind, whatever he said, and however he flattered, when he got me home to his house, he would sell me for a slave." Ah! it is even so. If we give way to any of the lusts of the flesh, we become slaves to them, and there is no slavery at all equal to that of the man who has given himself up to his own corrupt nature. He will go from bad to worse, and from worst to the very worst of all. What slavery drink involves! "Who hath woe? who hath sorrow? who hath contentions? who hath babbling? who hath wounds without cause? who hath redness of eyes? They that tarry long at the wine; they that go to seek mixed wine." As for our lusts, there are yet more glaring penalties which follow them. Every man knows that he cannot yield to them a little but the tendency is to yield to them more.

Thereupon, Old Adam began to revile Faithful. As surely as you resist the enticements of the flesh, it will turn and rend you. The devil has two ways of dealing with us. First he speaks us fair, and bids us do as he would; but if we say him "nay," he declares we are not children of God, and begins to rail at us as if he were himself a saint, and had a right to find fault with us. He will be our enemy in one direction or another. So did this old man to Faithful.

He did also another thing, which some of us understand very well. He gave Faithful a deadly twitch. Ah! it should bring tears into our eyes to recollect what twitches sin has sometimes given us, as though it would drag us into its thrall again. We knew the evil, and, by God's grace, resolved against it; nor did we fall into it, yet our feet were almost gone, our steps had well-nigh slipped. The flesh of the best of men is but the flesh of a depraved nature, and the old nature of the most holy man is thoroughly carnal, and cannot be otherwise. It is so bad and detestable that it must be buried, for even God Himself will never attempt to improve it. The new nature must come, and first subdue it, and ultimately mortify it, till it dies outright; but while it is there, it "is enmity against God," and "is not subject to the law of God, neither indeed can be." What twitches it can give, as though it would pull a man in two!

Many believers are greatly cast down because of this conflict within them. As soon as there are wars and fightings between the two men,—the old man and the new man,—they conclude at once that it is all over with them. Foolish conclusion, indeed! since, if there were no wars, it would be a proof that there was no life. If there were no conflicts, it would be an evidence that there was but one power within, and that power the evil one. Draw not from your internal commotions, from the temptation which assails you, and the force with which it acts against your inward principles,—draw not the inference that, therefore, you are a cast-away of God. This is rather a reason why you should cry, "Who shall deliver me from the body of this death?" and by faith should shout, "I thank God through Jesus Christ our Lord."

I have often been astounded at some Christians, who cannot understand anything about these inward conflicts resulting from this double nature. Real disciples though they doubtless are, they seem quite amazed that we should think it possible that the Christian should have in him his old corruptions. I may be worse than other people, but I am obliged to confess to you that never a day passes in which I am not painfully conscious of the sin that dwelleth in me; and though I know that I am saved by grace, and have a new nature wrought in me by God the Holy Spirit, yet I often have to call out, with the Apostle, "O wretched man that I am! who shall deliver me from the body of this death?" I thought that this was the experience of all God's people. I can only say that, if it could be dispensed with, I should be glad to be rid of it; but I believe that, up to the very gates of Heaven, there will be this daily conflict, this hourly struggle between the house of David and the house of Saul, between the seed of the woman and the seed of the serpent, between the Old Adam and the New Adam, between the natural and the spiritual.

However, our Pilgrim escaped; yet he escaped only with a threatening, for the old man told him that he would send one after him that should make his way bitter to his soul. You know who this was. It was Moses; for, when the law comes home to a Christian's conscience, it says to him, "You profess to have clean escaped from the corruption that is in the world through lust, but look at you! You know that, if you had been left to yourself, you would have done as others did; and though you have been kept from the actual sin, yet how you rolled the thought of it under your tongue, and how sweet it was! How can there be a change in your nature when such a thing can be said of you?" Down comes the great bludgeon again and again, till you lie all bleeding and ready to perish. When the law begins to deal even with a Christian, if One does not come by to aid him, it will soon slay the best among us. "By the deeds of the law there shall no flesh be justified in His sight." When the Christian comes to be judged by the law of God, it makes him say, "The law is spiritual: but I am carnal, sold under sin." It makes a man lie as though he were dead. "For I was alive without the law once; but when the commandment came, sin revived, and I died." I felt the power of sin working in me, and I seemed to lie, at the feet of the accuser, like one utterly devoid of life. Now, the law cannot really kill the Christian. If Christians know how to stand their ground, it will not harm them. We are not under the law, but under grace. We have not received the spirit of bondage again to fear; but we have received the Spirit of adoption, whereby we cry, "Abba, Father."

Moses is a good friend of ours, after all. He beats us very furiously; but, when he drives us to Christ, it is a blessed experience for us. If he threatens to burn down our house over our heads, if he drives us out of our refuges of lies, it is indeed a mercy for us. Nevertheless, for the conscience to be beaten by Moses, is a very painful process.

How joyful is the moment when He comes by who has "holes in His hands, and in His side"! Now, Christian, you understand that. When you get a sight of Christ crucified, Sinai's thunders cease to frighten. When you can feel that He loved you, and gave Himself for you, and bore the transgression of your Old Adam nature in His own body on the tree, you can rejoice with joy unspeakable, and full of glory. You know what it is to be knocked about by Moses. I trust you also know what it is to be healed by the loving Lord, and to be sent on your way rejoicing.

Some persons will not understand all this. I can only pray that they may yet do so; for, recollect that, if there be in you no strivings after that which is good, then you are altogether corrupt. If you are never disturbed, and never troubled, you have good cause to be distressed. If you never fight the battle, you will never win the victory. If you never suffer, you will never reign. If you have not learned to deny yourselves, you shall not be partakers with God's people. You can easily tell which of the fish in a river are dead, and which are alive. There is one floating down the stream on the top of the water. We may be certain that it is dead. But see you that other fish coming swiftly against the strong current? That is not a dead fish, but a living one. And when you find a man carried along by the customs of his neighbors, doing just as others are doing, you may conclude that is a dead soul. But when a man is fighting against himself, against custom, against everything that is of this world, then you may know that he is a living man, and the God who has given him life will sustain that life, and reward it at the last. The evidence of life is simple confidence in the bleeding Saviour. Beloved, keep your eyes on Him. He alone can guard you from Moses and from Adam the First. And, O poor sinner! if thou wouldst get perfect rest, turn thy tearful eyes to Him who says, "Look unto Me, and be ye saved, all the ends of the earth."

XIV.

VANITY FAIR.

"Then I saw in my dream, that when they were got out of the wilderness, they presently saw a town before them, and the name of that town is Vanity; and at the town there is a fair kept, called Vanity Fair. It is kept all the year long. It beareth the name of Vanity Fair, because the town where it is kept is lighter than vanity (Psa. lxii. 9), and also, because all that is there sold, or that cometh thither, is vanity; as it is the saying of the wise, "All that cometh is vanity' (Eccl. xi. 8)."

THE happiest state of a Christian is the holiest state. As there is most heat nearest to the sun, so there is most happiness nearest to Christ. No Christian enjoys comfort when his eyes are fixed on vanity. I do not blame ungodly men for rushing to their pleasures. Let them have their fill. That is all they have to enjoy, but Christians must seek their delights in a higher sphere than the insipid frivolities of the world. Vain pursuits are dangerous to renewed souls.

"Now, as I said, the way to the Celestial City lies just through this town where this lusty fair is kept; and he that would go to the city, and yet not go through this town, 'must needs go out of the world' (1 Cor. v. 10)."

When weary of the strife and sin that meets you on every hand, consider that all the saints have endured the same trial. They were not carried on beds of down to heaven, and you must not expect to travel more easily than they. They had to hazard their lives unto the death in the high places of the field, and you will not be crowned till you also have endured hardness as a good soldier of Jesus Christ. Therefore, "stand fast in the faith, quit you like men, be strong."

"Now these pilgrims, as I said, must needs go through this fair. Well, so they did; but, behold, even as they entered into the fair, all the people in the fair were moved, and the town itself, as it were, in a hubbub about them, and that for several reasons: For,

"First, The pilgrims were clothed with such kind of raiment as was diverse from the raiment of any that traded in that fair. The people, therefore, of the fair made a great gazing upon them! some said they were fools; some, they were bedlams; and some they were outlandish men (1 Cor. iv. 9).

"Secondly, And as they wondered at their apparel, so they did likewise at their speech; for few could understand what they said. They naturally spoke the language of Canaan; but they that kept the fair were the men of this world. So that from one end of the fair to the other, they seemed barbarians each to the other (1 Cor. ii. 7, 8)."

If you follow Christ fully you will be sure to be called by some ill name or other. They will say how singular you are. If you become a true Christian you will soon be a marked man. They will say, "How odd he is!" "How singular she is!" They will think that we try to make ourselves remarkable, when in fact, we are only conscientious, and are endeavoring to obey the will of God.

They will say, "Why you are old-fashioned!" You believe the same old things that they used to believe in Oliver Cromwell's day—those old Puritanical doctrines. They laugh at our faith and assert that we have lost our liberty.

"This fair is no new erected business, but a thing of ancient standing. I will show you the original of it.

"Almost five thousand years ago there were pilgrims walking to the Celestial City, as these two honest persons are; and Beelzebub, Apollyon, and Legion, with their companions, perceiving by the path that the pilgrims made, that their way to the city lay through this town of Vanity, they contrived here to set up a fair; a fair wherein should be sold all sorts of vanity, and that it should last all the year long. Therefore at this fair are all such merchandise sold as houses, lands, trades, places, honours, preferments, titles, countries, kingdoms, lusts, pleasures; and delights of all sorts, as harlots, wives, husbands, children, masters, servants' lives, blood, bodies, souls, silver, gold, pearls, precious stones, and what not. "

There are divers kinds of vanity. The cap and bells of the fool, the mirth of the world, the dance, the lyre, and the cup of the dissolute; all these men know to be vanities. They wear upon their forefront their proper name and title. Far more treacherous are those equally vain things, the cares of this world, and the deceitfulness of riches. A man may follow vanity as truly in the counting-house, as in the theatre. If he be spending his life in amassing wealth, he passes his days in a vain show. Unless we follow Christ, and make our God the great object of life, we only differ in appearance from the most frivolous.

It is the sweetness of sin that makes it the more dangerous. Satan never sells his poisons naked; he always gilds them before he vends them. Beware of pleasures. Many of them are innocent and healthful, but many are destructive. It is said that where the most beautiful cacti grow, there the most venomous serpents lurk. It is so with sin. Your fairest pleasures will harbour your grossest sins. Take care! Cleopatra's asp was introduced in a basket of flowers. Satan offers to the drunkard the sweetness of the intoxicating cup. He gives to each of us the offer of our peculiar joy; he tickleth us with pleasures, that he may lay hold of us.

"And moreover, at this fair, there are at all times to be seen jugglings, cheats, games, plays, fools, apes, knaves, and rogues, and that of every kind.

"Here are to be seen, too, and that for nothing, thefts,

murders, adulteries, false swearers, and that of a blood-red colour."

Banish for ever all thought of indulging the flesh if you would live in the power of your risen Lord. It were ill that a man who is alive in Christ should dwell in the corruption of sin. "Why seek ye the living among the dead?" said the angel to Magdalene. Should the living dwell in the sepulchre? Should divine life be immured in the charnel-house of fleshly lust? How can we partake of the cup of the Lord and yet drink the cup of Belial? Surely, believer, from open lusts and sins you are delivered; have you also escaped from the more secret and delusive lime-twigs of the Satanic fowler? Have you come forth from the lust of pride? Have you escaped from slothfulness? Have you clean escaped from carnal security? Are you seeking day by day to live above worldliness, the pride of life, and the ensnaring vice of avarice? Follow after holiness; it is the Christian's crown and glory.

"Thirdly, But that which did not a little amuse the merchandisers was, that these pilgrims set very light by all their wares. They cared not so much as to look upon them: and if they called upon them to buy, they would put their fingers in their ears, and cry, 'Turn away mine eyes from beholding vanity,' and look upwards signifying that their trade and traffic was in heaven (Phil. iii. 20, 21).

"One chanced, mockingly, beholding the carriage of the men to say unto them, 'What will ye buy?' But they, looking gravely upon him said, 'We buy the truth.' "

The common religion of the day is a mingle-mangle of Christ and Belial.

"If God be God serve Him; if Baal be God, serve him." There can be no alliance between the two. Jehovah and Baal can never be friends. "Ye cannot serve God and Mammon." "No man can serve two masters." All attempts at compromise in matters of truth and purity are founded on falsehood. May God save us from such hateful double-mindedness. You must have no fellowship with the unfruitful works of darkness, but rather reprove them. Walk worthy of your high calling and dignity. Remember, O Christian, that thou art a son of the King of kings. Therefore keep thyself unspotted from the world. Soil not the fingers which are soon to sweep celestial strings; let not those eyes becomes the windows of lust which are soon to see the King in His beauty; let not those feet be defiled in miry places, which are soon to walk the golden streets; let not those hearts be filled with pride and bitterness which are ere long to be filled with heaven, and to overflow with ecstatic joy:—

> "Rise where eternal beauties bloom,
>   And pleasures all divine;

> Where wealth that never can consume,
> And endless glories shine!"

"At that there was an occasion taken to despise the men the more; some mocking, some taunting, some speaking reproachfully, and some calling upon others to smite them. At last things came to a hubbub and great stir in the fair, insomuch that all order was confounded. Now was word presently brought to the great one of the fair, who quickly came down, and deputed some of his most trusty friends to take those men into examination about whom the fair was almost overturned. So the men were brought to examination; and they that sat upon them asked whence they came, whither they went, and what they did there in such an unusual garb. The men told them that they were pilgrims and strangers in the world, and that they were going to their own country, which was the heavenly Jerusalem, and that they had given no occasion to the men of the town, nor yet to the merchandisers, thus to abuse them, and to let them in their journey, except it was for that, when one asked them what they would buy, they said they would buy the truth. But they that were appointed to examine them, did not believe them to be any other than bedlams and mad, else such as came to put all things into a confusion in the fair. Therefore they took them and beat them, and besmeared them with dirt, and then put them into a cage, that they might be made a spectacle to all the men of the fair. There, therefore, they lay for some time, and were made the objects of any man's sport, or malice, or revenge; the great one of the fair laughing still at all that befell them."

Pilgrims travel as suspected persons through Vanity Fair. Not only are we under surveillance, but there are more spies than we reck of. The espionage is everywhere, at home and abroad. If we fall into the enemies' hands we may sooner expect generosity from a wolf, or mercy from a fiend, than anything like patience with our infirmities from men who spice their infidelity towards God with scandals against His people. Live a godly gracious life, and you will not escape persecution. You may be happily circumstanced so as to live among earnest Christians and so escape persecution; but take the average Christian man, and he will have a hard time of it if he is faithful. The ungodly will revile those who are true to the Lord Jesus. Christians are ridiculed in the workshop, they are pointed out in the street, and an opprobrious name is hooted at them. Now we shall know who are God's elect, and who are not. Persecution acts as a winnowing fan, and those who are light as chaff are driven away by its blast; but those who are true corn remain, and are purified. Careless of man's esteem, the truly God-fearing man holds on his way, and fears the Lord for ever.

"Let us hear the conclusion of the whole matter." My longing is that the churches may be more holy. I grieve to see so much of worldly conformity. How often wealth leads men astray; how many Christians follow the fashion of this wicked world. Alas! with all my preaching, many wander, and try to be members of the Church, and citizens of the world too. We have among us avowed lovers of Christ, who act too much like "lovers of pleasure."

It is a shameful thing for a professor of Christianity to be found in those music-halls, saloons, and places of revelry where you cannot go without your morals being polluted, for you can neither open your eyes nor your ears without knowing at once that you are in the purlieus of Satan.

I charge you by the living God, if you cannot keep good company, and avoid the circle of dissipation, do not profess to be followers of Christ, for He bids you come out from among them and be separate. If you can find pleasure in lewd society and lascivious songs, what right have you to mingle with the fellowship of saints or to join in the singing of psalms?

Keep the best company. Be much with those who are much with God. Let them be thy choicest companions who have made Christ their choicest companion; let Christ's love be thy love. With whom shall believers be, but believers? Our English proverb says, "Birds of a feather flock together." To see a saint and a sinner associating is to see the living and the dead keeping house together. It is better to be with Lazarus in rags, than with Dives in robes. Dwell where God dwells. Make those your companions on earth, who will be your companions in heaven.

An unholy Church! it is useless to the world, and of no esteem among men. It is an abomination, hell's laughter, heaven's abhorrence. The worst evils which have ever come upon the world have been brought upon her by an unholy Church. O Christian, the vows of the Lord are upon you. You are God's priest: act as such. You are God's king: reign over your lusts. You are God's chosen: do not associate with Belial. Heaven is your portion: live like a heavenly spirit. So shall you prove that you have true faith in Jesus, for there cannot be faith in the heart unless there be holiness in the life:

> "Lord, I desire to live as one
>   Who bears a blood-bought name;
> As one who fears but grieving Thee,
>   And knows no other shame."

XV.

"BEWARE OF THE FLATTERER."

WHEN Christian and Hopeful left the Delectable Mountains to pursue their way towards the Celestial City the shepherds bade them "Beware of the Flatterer." They learned afterwards, by sad experience, the folly of neglecting this advice, for thus the story runs:—

"They went then till they came at a place where they saw a way put itself into their way, and seemed withal to lie as straight as the way which they should go: and here they knew not which of the two to take, for both seemed straight before them; therefore, here they stood still to consider. And as they were thinking about the way, behold a man, black of flesh, but covered with a very light robe, came to them, and asked them why they stood there. They answered, they were going to the Celestial City, but knew not which of these ways to take. 'Follow me,' said the man, 'it is thither that I am going.' So they followed him in the way that but now came into the road, which by degrees turned, and turned them so from the city that they desired to go to, that, in little time, their faces were turned away from it; yet they followed him. But by-and-by, before they were aware, he led them both within the compass of a net, in which they were both so entangled, that they knew not what to do; and with that the white robe fell off the black man's back. Then they saw where they were. Wherefore there they lay crying some time, for they could not get themselves out.

"Then said Christian to his fellow, Now do I see myself in an error. Did not the shepherds bid us beware of the flatterers? As is the saying of the wise man, so we have found it this day, 'A man that flattereth his neighbour spreadeth a net for his feet.' (Prov. xxix. 5.)

"HOPE. They also gave us a note of directions about the way, for our more sure finding thereof; but therein we have also forgotten to read, and have not kept ourselves from the paths of the destroyer. Here David was wiser than we; for, saith he, concerning the works of men, 'By the word of Thy lips I have kept me from the paths of the destroyer.' (Psalm xvii. 4.)

"Thus they lay bewailing themselves in the net."

This is not a picture of a temptation to turn aside altogether from the good way. The path of the destroyer appeared to run parallel to that in which they ought to have kept. Nor did they go blundering on, but consulted with one another. Therein they were mistaken, for they should have consulted their Book of instructions. Then they were misled by a gentleman of pleasing appearance, who looked like a servant of the King of kings, and who spoke softly to them, assuring them that, as he himself was bound for the Celestial City, he could lead them thither. His winning accents caused them to yield themselves to his guidance; and, by-and-by, their faces were turned directly away from the city towards which aforetime they had been pressing. You see, it is not a case of the deliberate choice of sin; but rather of being deluded through neglect of the Word of God, which is the true guide of the pilgrim.

There are flatterers of this kind in our own hearts. It has often happened, in our experience, that we have been living in simple dependence upon the Lord Jesus Christ, which is the straight and narrow way which leadeth unto life eternal, and, by-and-by, we have, perhaps, read the experience of some great man, and we think, "Well, it must be right to feel as he felt, to doubt as he doubted, to be tempest-tossed as he was." This is another road, and we begin to think that it is well to live by feeling. The flatterer does not tell us, in so many words, to give up faith in Christ alone. We should recognize him, and be shocked if he did that: but he insinuates that we may walk a little by our holy feelings. We are not now such infants as we used to be; we have grown in grace somewhat; we may now rely a little upon the past; there is not the same need to be daily hanging upon Christ; why not rest on what was enjoyed at conversion, and make up, if necessary, with some present frames and feelings, present power in prayer, or present usefulness in the Lord's work?

Mr. Flatterer knows well that, when we are most

sanctified, there is enough cause to weep over every day in our life. He knows that those who most resemble Jesus are very, very far from being quite like Him. There is much more cause to deplore our sinnership, than to admire our saintship. As we have received Christ Jesus the Lord, so must we walk in Him. Still we rely upon His merits alone. If you begin to walk by yourself even a little way, you will soon find that path leading you, insensibly, into such legality that you try, if not actually to save yourself, yet to keep yourself saved through the works of the law. In a very little time, the believer who does this will fall into the net. He will find the pangs of hell, as it were, get hold upon him; he will find trouble and sorrow. When a bird is caught in a net, it attempts to get out this way and that way. It may break its wings, but it cannot escape; it rather entangles itself more completely. So the soul, that has forsaken simple faith, to live upon its own works, and feelings, and experiences, will try in vain to get relief. It is in legal bondage. The Ten Commandments suffice to make a heavy net when they twist around the sinner who has broken them. Apart from the blood of Jesus Christ, who can hope to escape from an awakened conscience? Thus is the Christian caught in a net when the Flatterer, who lives in his soul, tempts him to self-righteousness and to forsake the Lord. Luther used to say, "You need not fear a black devil half so much as a white one." The white devil of self-righteousness is more dangerous to the Christian than even the black devil of open sin. When open sin tempts us, we know it to be sin, and we are helped to forsake it. But, oftentimes, the white devil seems to be an angel of light; and, under the garb of striving after sanctification, or aiming at perfection, we are tempted to leave our child-like confidence in our Lord. This way lies the net!

There are so many other nets that I should not care to have to count them. You young converts may meet with a person who will say to you, "I hear you are converted; I am glad of that, but where do you attend?" "Oh, So-and-so!" "Ah! you should not go there; it is very well for some things, but there are higher truths that you will never learn there; you should come with us, and hear how we can explain the prophecies to you;" and so, under the guise of desiring you to listen to prophetic truth, they will lead you into some new form of error.

Others will seek to win you to admire with them the splendours of outward forms and ceremonies. How many unwary ones have been thus allured to Ritualism and Romanism! Certain others will say, "Oh, you should not have a minister!" They cry down the Lord's Shepherds who are found on the Delectable Mountains, and urge you to go where everybody teaches everybody. They are *the* people of God; they are not a sect, though ten thousand times more bigoted than any sect that ever existed. Beware, I pray you, of any form of doctrine or practice which would lead you from the place where you were born to God, where you have been nurtured in Christ, where you have been made useful, and helped forward in the Divine life. There are certain sects that only live by stealing members from other churches, whereas the aim of a Christian church should be to win souls direct from the world. These flatterers, for they are generally such, will tell you that you are too experienced to sit under the ordinary ministry; you are much too useful, or too spiritual, to remain in such a congregation. If you hearken unto them, you will soon find that leanness has come into your soul, and that you are entangled in the net, for you have been drawn away from the truth as it is in Jesus by some creed of man's devising.

I would warn our young members especially against that form of faith which holds only half the Bible; against those who proclaim the Divine election, but ignore human responsibility, and who preach up high doctrine, but have little or nothing to say about Christian practice. I am persuaded that this is another net of the Flatterer, and many have I seen taken in it. They have ceased from all care about the souls of others, have become indifferent as to whether children were perishing or being saved, have settled on their lees, to eat the fat, and drink the sweet, and have come to think that this was all for which they were redeemed. Their compassions have failed; they have had no weeping eyes over perishing sinners; in fact, they have thought it a sign of being unsound to care about saving sinners at all. May God keep you from being flattered into this net, lest you become pierced through with many sorrows! To the Bible only you must look. Test every new idea with this touchstone: "To the law and to the testimony." Require a "Thus saith the Lord" from every flattering notion. The old Book is our infallible guide.

Now let us read the passage in which Bunyan describes the pilgrims' release from the net.

"At last they espied a Shining One coming towards them, with a whip of small cord in His hand. When He was come to the place where they were, He asked them whence they came, and what they did there. They told Him that they were poor pilgrims going to Zion, but were led out of their way by a black man, clothed in white, 'who bid us,' said they, 'follow him, for he was going thither too.' Then said He with the whip, 'It is Flatterer, a false apostle, that hath transformed himself into an angel of light.' (Prov. xxix. 5. Daniel xi. 32. 2 Cor. xi. 14, 15.) So He rent the net, and let the men out. Then said He to them, 'Follow Me, that I may set you in your way again.' So He led them back to the way which they had left to follow the Flatterer. Then He asked them, saying, 'Where did you lie last night?' They said, 'With the Shepherds, upon the Delectable Mountains.' He asked them then, if they had not of those Shepherds a note of direction for the way. They answered, 'Yes.' 'But did you, said he, 'when you were at a stand, pluck out and read your note?' They answered, 'No.' He asked them, 'Why?' They said they forgot. He asked, moreover, if the Shepherds did not bid them beware of the Flatterer. They answered, 'Yes; but we did not imagine,' said they, 'that this fine-spoken man had been he.' (Romans xvi. 18.)

"Then I saw in my dream, that He commanded them to lie down; which, when they did, He chastised them sore, to teach them the good way wherein they should walk (Deut. xxv. 2); and as He chastised them, He said, 'As many as I love, I rebuke and chasten: be zealous, therefore, and repent.' (Rev. iii. 19. 2 Chron. vi. 26, 27.) This done, He bid them go on their way, and take good heed to the other directions of the Shepherds. So they thanked Him for all His kindness, and went softly along the right way, singing,—

> " 'Come hither, you that walk along the way;
> See how the pilgrims fare that go astray!
> They catched are in an entangling net,
> 'Cause they good counsel lightly did forget:
> 'Tis true, they rescued were, but yet you see
> They're scourged to boot. Let this your caution be,' "

When a Christian gets into the net of self-righteousness, he is sure to be delivered because he belongs to the Lord, who will not suffer him to be destroyed. But the Shining One, who comes to deliver him out of the net, will certainly bring a scourge of small cords with Him, and will chasten him, again and again, till he is willing to walk humbly with his God. Alas! how soon we get high looks and a proud bearing! We dream that we need not come crouching at the cross-foot, as other sinners do. I heard one say that he had not prayed for forgiveness of sin for twelve months; he had had his sins forgiven years ago. But when the Lord gives us a good dose of bitters, and makes us drink of the waters of Marah, we ask to be washed as Peter did when he changed his mind, and said, "Lord, not my feet only, but also my hands and my head." Then we feel the need of the daily application of the precious blood, and we are willing to stand with the poor publican, and say, "God be merciful to me a sinner." We must be chastened to keep us low. A good old countryman, now in Heaven, said to me, as I was walking with him in the field where he was ploughing, many years ago, "Ah, Master Spurgeon! if I get one inch above the ground, I get that inch too high, and have to come down again." So shall we. We must cling to the faith that owns that

Christ is our All-in-all. If the flatterer leads us astray, woe will be unto us. So will it be, I believe, with Christian men and women who, having received a blessing in any church, are induced to turn aside from it. "As a bird that wandereth from her nest, so is a man that wandereth from his place." Many such have been well chastened, and have had to come back to their old church again, and have rejoiced once more to sit with the Lord's people with whom they had happy fellowship in days gone by.

XVI.

THE ENCHANTED GROUND.

AS the spiritual guide of the flock of God along the intricate mazes of experience, it is the duty of the Gospel minister to point out every turning of the road to Heaven, to speak concerning its dangers and its privileges, and to warn any whom he may suspect to be in a position peculiarly perilous. Now, there is a portion of the road which leadeth from the City of Destruction to the Celestial City, which has in it, perhaps, more dangers than any other part of the way. It doth not abound with lions; there are no dragons in it; it hath no dark woods, and no deep pitfalls; yet more seeming pilgrims have been destroyed in that portion of the road than anywhere else; and not even Doubting Castle, with all its host of bones, can show so many who have been slain there. It is the part of the road called The Enchanted Ground. John Bunyan thus pictured it:—

"I saw them in my dream, that they went on till they came into a certain country, whose air naturally tended to make one drowsy, if he came a stranger into it. And here Hopeful began to be very dull and heavy of sleep; wherefore he said unto Christian, 'I do now begin to grow so drowsy that I can scarcely hold up mine eyes; let us lie down here, and take one nap.'

"CHR.   By no means, said the other; lest, sleeping, we never awake more.

"HOPE.   Why, my brother?   Sleep is sweet to the labouring man; we may be refreshed if we take a nap.

"CHR.   Do you not remember that one of the Shepherds bid us beware of the Enchanted Ground?   He meant by that, that we should beware of sleeping; 'therefore let us not sleep, as do others; but let us watch and be sober' (1 Thess. v. 6)."

There are, no doubt, many of us who are passing over this plain; and I fear that this is the condition of the majority of churches in the present day.   They are lying down on the settles of Lukewarmness in the Arbours of the Enchanted Ground.   There is not that activity and zeal we could wish to see among them; they are not, perhaps, notably heterodox; they may not be invaded by the lion of persecution; but they are lying down to slumber, like Heedless and Too-bold in the Arbour of Sloth.   God grant that His servants may be the means of arousing the Church from its lethargy, and stirring it up from its slumbers, lest haply, professors should sleep the sleep of death!

Let me picture to you the state of a sleeping Christian.

When a man is asleep, *he is insensible.*   The world moves on, and he knows nought about it.   The watchman calls out beneath his window, but he hears him not. A fire is raging in a neighbouring street, or his neighbour's house is burned to ashes; but he is asleep, and is unaware of the calamity. Persons are sick in the house where he lives, but he is not awakened; they may die, yet he weeps not for them. A revolution may be in progress in the streets of his city; a king may be losing his crown; but he that is asleep shares not in the turmoil of politics. A volcano may burst somewhere near him, and he may be in imminent peril; but he knows no fear; he is sound asleep, he is unconscious. The winds are howling, the thunders are rolling across the sky, and the lightnings flash past his window; but he who can sleep on careth for none of these things; he is insensible to them all. The sweetest music is echoing through the street; but he sleeps, and only in dreams doth he hear the sweetness. The most terrific wailings may assail his ears; but sleep has sealed them with the wax of slumber, and he hears not. Let the world break in sunder, and the elements go to ruin, keep him asleep, and he will not perceive it.

Slumbering Christian, behold a picture of your condition. Have you not sometimes mourned your insensibility? You wished you could feel; but all you felt was pain because you could not feel. You wished you could pray. It was not that you felt prayerless, but that you did not feel at all. You used to sigh once; you would give a world if you could sigh now. You used to groan once; a groan now would be worth a golden star if you could buy it. As for worldly songs, you can sing them, but your heart does not go with them. You go to the house of God; but when the multitude, that keep holy day, in the full tide of song send their music up to Heaven, you hear it, but your heart does not leap at the sound. Prayer goeth solemnly up to God's throne, like the smoke of the evening sacrifice; once, you could pray, too; but, now, while your body is in the house of God, your heart is elsewhere. You have become like a formalist; you feel that there is not that savour, that unction, in the preaching, that there used to be. There is no difference in your minister, you know; the change is in yourself. The hymns and the prayers are just the same, but you have fallen into a state of slumber. Once, if you thought of a man being damned, you felt as if you could weep your very soul out in tears; but, now, you could sit at the very brink of hell, and hear its wailings unmoved. Once, the thought of restoring a sinner from the error of his ways would have made you start from your bed at midnight, and you would have rushed through the cold air to help to rescue a sinner. Now, talk to you about perishing multitudes, and you hear it as an old, old tale. Tell you of thousands swept by the mighty flood of sin onwards to the precipice of destruction, you express your regret, you give your contribution, but your heart is not stirred within you. You must confess that you are insensible,—not entirely so, perhaps; but far too much so. You want to be awake, but you groan because you feel yourself to be in this state of slumber.

Again, sleep is a *state of inaction.* No daily bread is earned by him that sleepeth. The man who is stretched upon his couch neither writeth books, nor tilleth the ground, nor plougheth the sea, nor doeth aught else. His pulse beateth, so he is alive; but he is practically dead as to activity. Alas, beloved! this is the state of many of you. How many Christians are inactive! Once, it was their delight to instruct the young in the Sabbath-school; but that is given up. Once, they attended the early prayer-meeting, but they do not go there now. Once, they would be hewers of wood and drawers of water; but, alas! they are asleep now. Am I talking of what may possibly happen? Is it not too true almost universally? Are not the churches asleep? Where are the ministers who really preach? We have men who read essays, but is that preaching? We have men who can amuse an audience for twenty minutes, but is that preaching? Where

are the men who preach their very hearts out, and put
their souls into every sentence? Where are the men
who make it, not a profession, but a vocation, the
breath of their bodies, the marrow of their bones, the
delight of their spirits? Where are the Whitefields
and Wesleys now? Where are the Rowland Hills
now, who preached every day, and three times a day,
and were not afraid of preaching everywhere the un-
searchable riches of Christ? Brethren, the church
slumbers. It is not merely that the pulpit is a sentry-
box with the sentinel fast asleep; but the pews are
affected also. Why are the prayer-meetings almost
universally neglected? Where is the spirit of prayer,
where the life of devotion? Is it not almost extinct?
Are not our churches "fallen, fallen, fallen, from their
high estate"? God wake them up, and send them
more earnest and praying men!

The man who is asleep is also *in a state of insecurity.*
The murderer smiteth him that sleeps; the midnight
robber plundereth the house of him that resteth list-
lessly on his pillow. Jael smiteth a sleeping Sisera.
Abishai taketh away the spear from the bolster of a
slumbering Saul. A sleeping Eutychus falleth from
the third loft, and is taken up dead. A sleeping
Samson is shorn of his locks, and the Philistines are
upon him. Sleeping men are ever in danger; they

cannot ward off the blow of the enemy, nor strike in their own defense. Christian, if thou art sleeping, thou art in danger. Thy life, I know, can never be taken from thee, for it is hid with Christ in God. But, oh! thou mayest lose thy spear from the bolster; thou mayest lose much of thy faith; and thy cruse of water, wherewith thou dost moisten thy lips, may be stolen by the prowling thief. Thou little knowest thy danger. Awake, thou slumberer! Start up from the place where thou now liest in thine insecurity. This is not the sleep of Jacob, in which a ladder unites Heaven and earth, and angels tread the ascending rounds; but this is the sleep in which ladders are raised from hell, and devils climb upward from the pit to seize thy slumbering spirit.

Sleepy Christian, let me shout in thine ears,—thou art sleeping while souls are being lost,—sleeping while men are being damned,—sleeping while hell is being peopled,—sleeping while Christ is being dishonoured, —while the devil is grinning at thy sleepy face,— sleeping while demons are dancing round thy slumbering carcass, and telling it in hell that a Christian is asleep. You will never catch the devil asleep; let not the devil catch you asleep. Watch, and be sober, that ye may be always ready to do your duty.

A Christian is most liable to sleep when his tem-

poral circumstances are all right. When your nest is well feathered, you are then most likely to sleep; there is little danger of your sleeping when there is a bramble bush in the bed. When your couch is downy, then the most likely thing for you to say will be, "Soul, thou hast much goods laid up for many years; take thine ease, eat, drink, and be merry." Let me ask some of you,—when you were more straitened in circumstances, when you had to rely upon providence each hour, and had troubles to take to the throne of grace, were you not more wakeful than you are now? The miller, who hath his wheel turned by a constant stream, goes to sleep; but he that dependeth on the wind, which sometimes bloweth hard and sometimes gently, sleeps not, lest haply the full gust might rend the sails, or there should not be enough to make them go round. Easy roads tend to make us slumber. Few sleep in a storm; many sleep on a calm night. Why is the church asleep now? She would not sleep if Smithfield were filled with stakes, if St. Bartholomew's tocsin were ringing in her ears; she would not sleep if Sicilian Vespers might be sung on to-morrow's eve; she would not sleep if massacres were common now. But what is her condition? Every man sitting under his own vine and fig tree, none daring to make him afraid. Tread softly, she is fast asleep!

Another dangerous time is *when all goes well in spiritual matters.* You do not read that Christian went to sleep when lions were in the way, nor when he was passing through the river of death, nor when he was in Giant Despair's castle, nor during his fight with Apollyon. Poor creature! he almost wished he *could* sleep then. But when he had got half way up the Hill Difficulty, and came to a pretty little arbour, in he went, and sat down and began to read his roll. Oh, how he rested himself! How he unstrapped his sandals, and rubbed his weary feet! Very soon his mouth was open, his arms hung down, and he was fast asleep. Again, the Enchanted Ground was a very easy smooth place, and liable to send the pilgrim to sleep. You remember Bunyan's description of one of the arbours:—

"Then they came to an arbour, warm, and promising much refreshing to the Pilgrims; for it was finely wrought above head, beautified with greens, furnished with benches and settles. It also had in it a soft couch, whereon the weary might lean. . . This arbour was called The Slothful's Friend, on purpose to allure, if it might be, some of the pilgrims there to take up their rest when weary."

Depend upon it, it is in easy places that men shut their eyes, and wander into the dreamy land of forgetfulness. Old Erskine said a good thing when he remarked, "I like a roaring devil better than a sleeping devil." There is no temptation half so bad as not being tempted. The distressed soul does not sleep; it is after we get into confidence and full assurance that we are in danger of slumbering. Take care, thou who art full of gladness. There is no season in which we are so likely to fall asleep as that of high enjoyment. Take heed, joyous Christian, good frames are very dangerous; they often lull into sound slumber.

One of the most likely places for us to sleep in is *when we get near our journey's end.* The pilgrims' guide said to Christiana :—

"This Enchanted Ground is one of the last refuges that the enemy to pilgrims has. Wherefore it is, as you see, placed almost at the end of the way, and so it standeth against us with the more advantage. For when, thinks the enemy, will these fools be so desirous to sit down, as when they are weary? and when so like to be weary, as when almost at their journey's end? Therefore it is, I say, that the Enchanted Ground is placed so nigh to the Land Beulah, and so near the end of their race. Wherefore, let pilgrims look to themselves, lest it happen to them as it has done to these, that, as you see, are fallen asleep, and none can wake them."

It is quite true, that those, who have been for years in grace, are most in danger of slumbering. Somehow, we get into the routine of religious observance; it is customary for us to go to the house of God, it is usual for us to belong to the church, and that of itself tends to make people sleepy. If we are always going along the same road, we are liable to sleep. If Moab gets at ease, and is not emptied from vessel to vessel, he sleeps on, for he knows no change; and when years have worn our road with a rut of godliness, we are apt to throw the reins on our horse's neck, and sleep soundly.

What is to be done to ensure wakefulness when crossing the Enchanted Ground? One of the best plans is to *keep Christian company, and talk about the ways of the Lord.*

Christian said to Hopeful, "To prevent drowsiness in this place, let us fall into good discourse."

"With all my heart," said Hopeful.

"Where shall we begin?" asked Christian.

"Where God began with us," replied his companion.

There is no subject so likely to keep a godly man awake as talking of the place where God began with him. When Christian men talk together, they won't fall asleep together. Keep Christian company, and you will not be so likely to slumber. Christians, who isolate themselves, and stand alone, are very liable to lie down on the settle or the soft couch, and go to sleep; but if you talk much together, as they did in the olden time, you will find it extremely beneficial. Two Christians talking together of the ways of the Lord

MR. FEARING

"Here also he stood a good while before he would adventure to knock."

XVII.

HOW MR. FEARING FARED.

SOME of you know Mr. Fearing very well, for he has lived in your house, and perhaps he is even a very near relative of yours. When Mr. Great-heart, who represents the minister of Christ who is well taught, and strong in grace, was walking along with Father Honest, who stands for an aged, experienced, sober-minded Christian, John Bunyan tells us :—

"The guide asked the old gentleman, if he did not know one Mr. Fearing, that came on pilgrimage out of his parts.

"Hon. Yes, very well, said he. He was a man that had the root of the matter in him; but he was one of the most troublesome pilgrims that ever I met with in all my days."

This is an exact description of many who are on the road to Heaven. They are thoroughly sincere, nobody can doubt that; but they are "so nervous." I think that is how they describe themselves. "So doubtful, so mistrustful, so suspicious, so over-loaded with doubts and fears," would, perhaps, be a truer verdict. What wonder, then, that they are amongst "the most troublesome pilgrims" that you can meet with? Bunyan gives us a further dialogue concerning Mr. Fearing:—

"GREAT-HEART.   I perceive you knew him; for you have given a very right character of him.

"HON.   Knew him! I was a great companion of his; I was with him most an end; when he first began to think of what would come upon us hereafter, I was with him.

"GREAT-HEART.   I was his guide from my Master's house to the gates of the Celestial City.

"HON.   Then you knew him to be a troublesome one.

"GREAT-HEART.   I did so, but I could very well bear it; for men of my calling are oftentimes entrusted with the conduct of such as he was."

The minister of Christ is not to think the most fearful to be the most troublesome; but as it is his employment to help the timid, and, instrumentally, deliver them from their distress, he should be glad to find out those feeble minds, and seek to do them a good turn for the Master's sake.

"HON.   Well then, pray let us hear a little of him, and how he managed himself under your conduct.

"GREAT-HEART.   Why, he was always afraid that he should come short of whither he had a desire to go."

This is a great fear which haunts many,—the fear lest, after all, they should be castaways, lest they should prove hypocrites, lest they should fall from grace, lest they should be tempted above what they are able to bear; lest, in some evil hour, they should be given up by God the Holy Spirit, or be deserted by the Lord Jesus, and so should fall into great sin, and ultimately perish. This is a fear which haunts tens of thousands.

"Everything frightened him that he heard anybody speak of, that had but the least appearance of opposition in it."

We meet with some such still. You cannot speak to them about the sorrows of the Christian's life but they say, "We shall never be able to bear these." If you refer to conflicts, they reply, "We are sure we shall never succeed in fighting our way to Heaven." If they hear of anybody who has backslidden, they exclaim, "That is just what we shall do; we are certain that is what will happen to us." If you have ever talked with these people, you know how difficult it is to describe them, for they are so gloomy that they seem to darken the sun even at noon-day.

"I hear that he lay roaring at the Slough of Despond for about a month together; nor durst he, for all he saw several go over before him, venture, though they, many of them, offered to lend him their hand."

Poor soul! There he lay "roaring", as Bunyan says; that is, sighing, crying, bemoaning himself. He could not pluck up courage to go across, but there he lay by the month together. Others came up, and went across safely, and offered to lend him their hand,

but it was no use. You may try to help these desponding ones, but you will need a wisdom superior to your
own to deal with them effectually, for it must be
admitted that they are wonderfully wilful although
they are very weak. While they are as incapable as
little children, they are also often as wilful as strong
men, and they will stick to their fears, do what you
will to drive them out of them. I have sometimes
gone a-hunting after these people; and when I have
dug them out of one hole, they have crept into another.
I have thought, "Now, I shall have you; I shall make
an end of your doubts this time;" but they have
sprung up in quite another quarter. They seem to
be most ingenious at inventing reasons for suspicion
concerning themselves. When everybody else can see
something that is good in them, they say, "Pray don't
flatter us; don't try to deceive us!"

"He would not go back again neither."

Ah, that is the best of it! Mr. Fearing will not go
back. There are some boastful ones, who set out
boldly enough, but they turn their backs in the day of
battle. Mr. Fearing goes very slowly, but he is very
sure. He will not go back; he knows there is no hope
for him there, so he will even go on a little further,
though he is half-afraid to venture.

"'The Celestial City,' he said, 'he should die if he came

not to it'; and yet was dejected at every difficulty, and stumbled at every straw that anybody cast in his way. Well, after he had lain at the Slough of Despond a great while, as I have told you, one sunshine morning, I do not know how, he ventured, and so got over; but when he was over, he would scarce believe it."

Just like him! It may be a very bright "sunshine morning" when some sweet promise enlightens his soul, when the Spirit of God comes to him like a dove, bearing comfort on His wings. Then the good man begins to feel unusually and extraordinarily strong for him, so he makes a dash, and gets through his trouble; but he can hardly believe that he has really got over it. He is quite sure that he shall sink now. When Mr. Fearing got out of the Slough, he could not understand how it was that he had done it. It must be amazing grace that had brought such a poor sinner as he was out of it, but he felt so unworthy that he was persuaded he would be cast away even then. He could scarcely believe in his heart that it was true. It was said of Peter, when the iron gate of the prison opened of its own accord, and he found himself in the street, "He wist not that it was true which was done by the angel; but thought he saw a vision." Just so, when Mr. Fearing does get a gleam of comfort, he thinks that it is too good to be true.

"He had, I think, a Slough of Despond in his mind; a

slough that he carried everywhere with him, or else he could never have been as he was. So he came up to the gate, you know what I mean, that stands at the head of this way; and there also he stood a good while before he would adventure to knock."

He would not venture to pray. He was overcome with fear at the very first stage of spiritual life. He had it in his heart to knock at mercy's gate, to use the means of grace, to enquire after Christ, but apprehension stayed his hand, and sealed his lips.

"When the gate was opened, he would give back, and give place to others and say that he was not worthy."

Others might go in, others might succeed, but *he* was quite unworthy. The poor soul was perfectly right. He was by no means worthy; but, then, *no one* is. We do not knock at the gate because we are worthy. When we give away alms, we like to bestow them on worthy persons; but our Lord Jesus Christ never found one yet who was worthy of His mercy, and therefore He takes care to give it to those unworthy ones who are ready to confess their need.

"For, for all he got before some to the gate, yet many of them went in before him. There the poor man would stand, shaking and shrinking. I dare say, it would have pitied one's heart to have seen him; nor would he go back again."

He was still afraid to pray, and could not think

that God would hear him; but he would groan and
cry, if he could not pray. Moreover, he would not go
back again. He could not refrain from using the
means of grace, though he could not think there was
any comfort in them for him. Still, he would not
neglect them. No matter though the prayer-meeting
did not cheer him, he would be present; and though
the sermon, he thought, could not be meant for such
as he was, yet still he would hear it. Oh! these are
strange drawings which the Lord puts into the hearts
of poor, melancholy, feeble-minded ones, so that He
draws them even against their own wills, and draws
them with a kind of despairing hope—or hopeful despair—right away from themselves to Christ!

"At last, he took the hammer that hanged on the gate in his
hand, and gave a small rap or two."

He dared not do more. It was only "a small rap
or two,"—something like this, "God be merciful to me
a sinner!" or, "Lord, save me!"

"Then one opened to him."

You see, the Lord does not make us all knock alike.
The strong ones may have to knock long before the
door is opened; but to the weak ones the door springs
open at the first tap. Master Bunyan tells us, in his
"Solomon's Temple Spiritualized," that the posts on

which the doors of the temple hung "were of the olive-tree, that fat and oily tree," so that the hinges would be kept well oiled; and when any poor soul came to enter the doors, they would swing open at once.

"Then one opened to him, but he shrank back as before. He that opened stepped out after him, and said, 'Thou trembling one, what wantest thou?' With that he fell down to the ground. He that spoke to him wondered to see him so faint. So he said to him, 'Peace be to thee; up, for I have set open the door to thee. Come in, for thou art blessed.' With that he got up, and went in trembling; and when he was in, he was ashamed to show his face."

Just such are these trembling ones. When they do get some kind of comfort and enjoyment, they are ashamed to show their faces. They are glad to get into the dark, and to sit in any quiet corner where nobody can observe them.

XVIII.

HOW MR. FEARING FARED.

(*Concluded.*)

"Well, after he had been entertained there a while, as you know how the manner is, he was bid go on his way, and also told the way he should take. So he came till he came to our house. But as he behaved himself at the gate, so he did at my Master the Interpreter's door. He lay thereabout in the cold a good while, before he would adventure to call; yet he would not go back; and the nights were long and cold then."

THIS is a still further advance. He was still seeking Christ, but now he had had some of the teaching of the Holy Spirit, and was beginning to understand something of the Gospel. Notice how that good word always comes in, "He would not go back." He was afraid even to receive the truths of God's Word as his own, and to take one gleam of comfort from them; yet he would not go back. He would linger at the door even if not admitted. Oh, the tenacity of grip which there is in the poor seeking sinner when he once gets some hold of the precious promises of Christ!

"Nay, he had a note of necessity in his bosom to my

Master, to receive him, and grant him the comfort of His house, and also to allow him a stout and valiant conductor, because he was himself so chicken-hearted a man; and yet, for all that, he was afraid to call at the door."

Bunyan here means that this poor man had a special and particular claim upon the Spirit of God for some full-grown Christian to help him on the road to Heaven. But for all that, he dared not speak to the minister. He was afraid of him. He felt himself quite unworthy to look at the good man.

"So he lay up and down thereabouts, till, poor man! he was almost starved. Yea, so great was his dejection, that though he saw several others, for knocking, get in, yet he was afraid to venture. At last, I think, I looked out of the window, and perceiving a man to be up and down about the door, I went out to him, and asked what he was; but, poor man! the water stood in his eyes; so I perceived what he wanted."

So you, who love Christ, and have some ability in instructing converts, should look after those that are too timid to look after you. You will often see these people going up and down. You will see them here, on Sunday, at the classes and the services. They sometimes want to be spoken to; and if the Holy Spirit has enlightened you, you should look out for them.

"I went, therefore, in, and told it in the house, and we shewed the thing to our Lord."

That is the way. If you cannot help them yourselves, go and tell the Lord about them. Go and pray to Him about these desponding ones, who will not avail themselves of the comforts which He has provided for them.

"So He sent me out again, to entreat him to come in; but, I dare say, I had hard work to do it. At last he came in; and I will say that for my Lord, He carried it wonderfully lovingly to him. There were but a few good bits at the table, but some of it was laid upon his trencher. Then he presented the note, and my Lord looked thereon, and said his desire should be granted."

Ah! when the poor soul does get to see what real comfort there is for it, it seems then as if the best things in the Word of God were meant for the feeblest saints, and as if the Lord had laid Himself out in a way of mercy to write the most precious conceivable words for those who are of a tender spirit, and go with broken bones.

"So when he had been there a good while, he seemed to get some heart, and to be a little more comfortable; for my Master, you must know, is one of very tender bowels, especially to them that are afraid; wherefore He carried it so towards him as might tend most to his encouragement. Well, when he had had a sight of the things of the place, and was ready to take his journey to go to the city, my Lord, as He did to Christian before, gave him a bottle of spirits, and some comfortable things to eat. Thus we set forward, and I went before him; but the man was but of few words, only he would sigh aloud."

This was a delicate task for Mr. Great-heart, but it is the task of many an advanced Christian. He must not shrink from it; and if he gets no instruction from the poor man, he must recollect that we are not always to be getting, but that sometimes we are to be giving as well.

"When we were come to where the three fellows were hanged, he said that he doubted that that would be his end also."

Of course, he could not look upon such a sight as that without fearing that, one day, he would be in a similar position. There never is a case of church examination or church censure but poor Mr. Fearing says, "Ah! I shall come to that some day;" and when he reads of Judas and Demas, he says, "Ah! that will surely be my fate."

"Only he seemed glad when he saw the Cross and the Sepulchre. There, I confess, he desired to stay a little to look, and he seemed, for a while after, to be a little cheery."

Well, if he was not happy there, where would he be? If the good man could not pluck up his courage sitting at the foot of the cross, where would he be of good cheer? It is delightful to notice how Bunyan picks out the comforting influence of the cross of Christ upon the most desponding spirit.

> "Sweet the moments, rich in blessing,
>   Which before the cross I spend."

"When we came at the Hill Difficulty, he made no stick at that, nor did he much fear the lions; for you must know that his trouble was not about such things as those; his fear was about his acceptance at last."

It is wonderful that these timid ones are often not afraid of the things which frighten others. Hardships do not trouble them. They could almost bear to be burned in the flames. They are not afraid of martyrdom, but they are afraid of sin and self,—a very healthy fear, but it must be coupled with a healthy faith in Christ, or else it becomes a very wretched thing.

"I got him in at the House Beautiful, I think, before he was willing."

That is, into the Christian church. Mr. Great-heart cheered him on, and got him to see the church-officers, and to unite with the church almost before he knew what he was at.

"Also, when he was in, I brought him acquainted with the damsels that were of the place; but he was ashamed to make himself much for company. He desired much to be alone, yet he always loved good talk, and often would get behind the screen to hear it."

This is just the state of mind in which many believers are after they have joined the church. They are bashful; they would not like to push themselves forward. They would rather lose many things than be thought to be at all impertinent or pushing.

"He also loved much to see ancient things, and to be pondering them in his mind."

I know he loved the precious doctrine of eternal love.

"He told me afterwards that he loved to be in those two houses from which he came last, to wit, at the gate, and that of the Interpreter, but that he durst not be so bold to ask.

"When we went also from the House Beautiful, down the Hill, into the Valley of Humiliation, he went down as well as ever I saw a man in my life; for he cared not how mean he was, so he might be happy at last. Yea, I think, there was a kind of sympathy betwixt that valley and him, for I never saw him better in all his pilgrimage than when he was in that valley. Here he would lie down, embrace the ground, and kiss the very flowers that grew in this valley. (Lam. iii. 27-29.) He would now be up every morning by break of day, tracing and walking to and fro in this valley."

Humility just suited him. He was a plant that could grow in the shade. You could not humble him too much, for that was just his element. He loved to feel his nothingness, and to be brought low, for then he felt himself safe. You see, Mr. Fearing has his quiet, peaceful, happy times. He can sing, "The Lord is my Shepherd; I shall not want. He maketh me to lie down in green pastures; He leadeth me beside the still waters."

That is a very happy state to be in, naturally fearful, but yet brought so low that you do not fear at all;

so sensible of your own weakness that you look wholly to superior strength, and therefore have no cause for fear.

"But when he was come to the entrance of the Valley of the Shadow of Death, I thought I should have lost my man; not for that he had any inclination to go back; that he always abhorred; but he was ready to die for fear. 'Oh! the hobgoblins will have me! the hobgoblins will have me!' cried he; and I could not beat him out on it. He made such a noise, and such an outcry here, that, had they but heard him, it was enough to encourage them to come and fall upon us.

"But this I took very great notice of, that this valley was as quiet while he went through it, as ever I knew it before or since. I suppose these enemies here had now a special check from our Lord, and a command not to meddle until Mr. Fearing was passed over it."

Bunyan here very wittily and pithily depicts the absurd fears of Mr. Fearing when there was no ground for fear. He makes "the hobgoblins" in his own imagination, and then cries out, "They will have me!" He thinks he will fall in this, or be cast away for that, or that God will forsake him. Oh! it is foolish to indulge such fears; yet many men are so weak that, all their lives long, they cannot escape from them.

"It would be too tedious to tell you of all. We will, therefore, only mention a passage or two more. When he

was come at Vanity Fair, I thought he would have fought
with all the men at the fair. I feared there we should both
have been knocked on the head, so hot was he against their
fooleries."

Mr. Fearing was only afraid that he should not be
safe at the last, but he was a bold fellow when he
came to deal with the enemies of the cross of Christ.
It is singular, this combination of bravery and
trembling. He trembles lest he should not be saved
at last, but he strikes out at his enemies right and
left. You know what the "fooleries" were. There
was the foolery of old Rome, and Mr. Fearing could
not stand that, but would like to smash it all up.

"Upon the Enchanted Ground, he was also very wakeful."

Strong faith sometimes goes almost to sleep there.
We are apt to get presumptuous. We, who have many
comforts, get to think that it is all right with us. May
we, however, be kept awake! I would rather you
should go to Heaven doubting your interest in Christ
than that you should go to hell presuming that you
are safe when really you are not. It is a sad and
sinful thing to be always doubting; but, still, it is
infinitely better than to have a name to live while you
are dead.

"But when he was come at the river where was no bridge,
there again he was in a heavy case. Now, now, he said,

he should be drowned for ever, and so never see that face with comfort that he had come so many miles to behold.

"And here, also, I took notice of what was very remarkable; the water of that river was lower at this time than ever I saw it in all my life. So he went over at last, not much above wet-shod. When he was going up to the gate, I began to take my leave of him, and to wish him a good reception above. So he said, 'I shall, I shall.' Then parted we asunder, and I saw him no more."

He was afraid to die, poor man, not because he was afraid of death, but lest he should not see the face of Him whom he loved so much, but who, he almost feared, would reject him. Here, again, we see the abundant mercy of God, for Mr. Fearing did not sink in the deep waters, but he died easily and went over the river "not much above wet-shod," and his last words were, "I shall, I shall." Yes, and so you will, poor Mr. Fearing. You sometimes say that you shall not, but that is your unbelief. You shall; you shall; for the Master has said, "Him that cometh to Me I will in no wise cast out."

MR. GREAT-HEART

"So he took his weapons and went before them."

XIX.

MR. FEEBLE-MIND AND MR. READY-TO-HALT.

WHILE at the house of Gaius with the pilgrims, Mr. Great-heart and his companions went forth to the haunt of Giant Slay-good.

"When they came to the place where he was, they found him with one Feeble-mind in his hands, whom his servants had brought unto him, having taken him in the way. Now the giant was rifling him, with a purpose, after that, to pick his bones; for he was of the nature of flesh-eaters."

Out of the giant's hands Mr. Feeble-mind was delivered, and the giant himself was slain. Poor Mr. Feeble-mind! Let us read what he says about himself:—

"'I am a sickly man, as you see; and, because death did usually once a day knock at my door, I thought I should never be well at home; so I betook myself to a pilgrim's life, and have travelled hither from the town of Uncertain, where I and my father were born. I am a man of no strength at all of body, nor yet of mind; but would, if I could, though I can but crawl, spend my life in the pilgrim's way. When I came at the gate that is at the head of the way, the Lord of that place did entertain me freely; neither objected He against my weakly looks, nor against my feeble mind; but gave me such things as were necessary for my journey, and bid me hope to the end. When I came to the house of the Interpreter, I received much kindness there; and because the Hill Difficulty was judged too hard for me, I was carried up that by one of His servants. Indeed I have found much relief from pilgrims, though none were willing to go so softly as I am forced to do; yet still, as they came on, they bid me be of good cheer, and said that it was the will of their Lord that comfort should be given to the feeble-minded, and so went on their own pace. (1 Thess. v. 14.) When I was come up to Assault Lane, then this giant met with me, and bid me prepare for an encounter; but, alas! feeble one that I was, I had more need of a cordial. So he came up and took me. I conceited he should not kill me. Also, when he had got me into his den, since I went not with him willingly, I believed I should come out alive again; for I have heard, that not any pilgrim that is taken captive by violent hands, if he keeps heart-whole towards his Master, is, by the laws of Providence, to die by the hand of the enemy. Robbed I looked to be, and robbed to be sure I am; but I am, as you see, escaped with life; for the which I thank my King as author, and you as the means. Other brunts I also look for: but this I have resolved on, to wit, to run when I can, to go when I cannot run, and to creep when I cannot go. As to the main, I thank Him that loves me, I am fixed. My way is before me, my mind is beyond the river that has no bridge, though I am, as you see, but of feeble mind.'"

Poor soul! We know some just like him. It is not necessary to explain his condition, or to dwell on his adventure. We pass on to his later experiences.

The pilgrims tarried awhile at the house of Gaius,

and Feeble-mind got fattened up a bit; they had a glorious special meeting, and then Mr. Great-heart said it was time for the pilgrims to go on their journey again.

"Now Mr. Feeble-mind, when they were going out of the door, made as if he intended to linger; the which when Mr. Great-heart espied, he said, 'Come, Mr. Feeble-mind, pray do you go along with us, I will be your conductor, and you shall fare as the rest.'"

Mr. Great-heart, who is, of course, the minister, insisted that Mr. Feeble-mind should not leave the band of pilgrims. He wanted to go to Heaven without joining the church; and that the teacher could not sanction. But feeble as he was, he was a man of very choice mind. Sterner people can bear a little laughing, and they do not take so much notice of how silly people dress, and they can even bear a debate over the question; but poor Feeble-mind said:—

"'Alas! I want a suitable companion; you are all lusty and strong; but I, as you see, am weak; I choose, therefore, rather to come behind, lest, by reason of my many infirmities, I should be both a burden to myself and to you. I am, as I said, a man of a weak and feeble mind, and shall be offended and made weak at that which others can bear. I shall like no laughing; I shall like no gay attire; I shall like no unprofitable questions. Nay, I am so weak a man, as to be offended with that which others have a liberty to do. I do not yet know all the truth; I am a very ignorant Christian man; sometimes, if I hear any rejoice in the

Lord, it troubles me, because I cannot do so too. It is with me, as it is with a weak man among the strong, or as with a sick man among the healthy, or as a lamp despised. "He that is ready to slip with his feet, is as a lamp despised in the thought of him that is at ease," (Job. xii. 5,) so that I know not what to do.'

" 'But brother,' said Mr. Great-heart, 'I have it in commission to "comfort the feeble-minded," and to "support the weak." (1 Thess. v. 14.) You must needs go along with us; we will wait for you; we will lend you our help (Romans xiv. 1); we will deny ourselves of some things, both opinionative and practical, for your sake (1 Cor. viii.); we will not enter into doubtful disputations before you: we will be made all things to you, rather than you shall be left behind. (1 Cor. ix. 22.)' "

I want you to notice that the duty of the weak to join the church is here enjoined, and also that those with whom they join are to be gentle with them.

Here is a pretty piece of Mr. Bunyan's writing:—

"Now all this while they were at Gaius's door; and behold, as they were thus in the heat of their discourse, Mr. Ready-to-halt came by, with his crutches in his hand (Ps. xxxviii. 17); and he also was going on pilgrimage.

"Then said Mr. Feeble-mind to him, 'Man how camest thou hither? I was but just now complaining, that I had not a suitable companion, but thou art according to my wish. Welcome, welcome, good Mr. Ready-to-halt, I hope thou and I may be some help.'

" 'I shall be glad of thy company,' said the other; 'and, good Mr. Feeble-mind, rather than we will part, since we are thus happily met, I will lend thee one of my crutches.'

" 'Nay,' said he, 'though I thank thee for thy good will, I am not inclined to halt before I am lame.' "

See how he perks up at the very idea of it.

" 'Howbeit, I think, when occasion is, it may help me against a dog.' "

So, you see, he found congenial company in the church. The first thing for us to note is, that there are some poor feeble-minded saints who really are not nice company, but who must not be slighted. They are not very cheerful; they may not be even amiable; they have feeble minds; you will not learn much from them; they are, as Bunyan says, "very ignorant Christian men;" but we ought not, as a church, to hesitate to have these added to us, we should be glad that they come amongst us. I heard a person say, "Look what a number of very poor people are coming into the church," I am glad of it, they are the very people who need church-fellowship, and spiritual privileges. Besides, many of the poor of the earth are the excellent of the earth. Feeble-mind was a man of a very gracious and tender spirit. When he heard other people joking and making fun, it grated on his ear; he saw others dressed out, it might not have been to any great excess, but he judged it out of harmony with the Christian simplicity enjoined by the apostle Peter; and that grieved him. This and that, which a stronger saint could do and bear without any harm, hurt his sensitive disposition. He did not wish to be always picking holes in other people's coats; he thought, therefore, that he would walk to Heaven as best as he could alone.

Now, I like Mr. Great-heart's pressing him to come into the church. Mr. Great-heart was a strong man, with a sword and shield; and if anybody needed such a protector, it was surely Mr. Feeble-mind, who could not defend himself. We want the feeble in mind in this church;—I know they are not very desirable from one point of view; but, then, we are not very desirable ourselves, yet Christ came to seek and to save us. It is a desirable thing that we should be able to put up with these poor Feeble-minds. Do you not think we often get most out of those people who try us most? When a man tries our temper, and lets us know how bad it is, it is beneficial to us. If you have an invalid child, or a sick friend, you do not make a great noise, you learn to be quiet and considerate. Gentleness and tenderness are learned in this school. It is a good thing to have a weakly saint about, for it helps to make others tender. It is well for the church to have Feeble-minds in it, and there can be no doubt that it is good for the Feeble-minds to be in the church.

But do you see what Mr. Great-heart says to this feeble companion. He says, in effect, "We will wait for you; if you cannot run as we do, we will walk at your pace. We will not overdrive you." I know how it is with some Christians; they have grown in grace so wonderfully, that they want everybody to be up to their height, and not three-quarters of an inch below it. They hear some dear child of God groaning over his corruptions, and his trials in the Christian life, and they look at him as if he were one of the very worst of sinners, whereas it is a thousand to one that the tried believer is a better saint than he who is hectoring and boasting. The boaster is like a rough boy who has a sweet, little, delicate sister, who is worth ten of him; she cannot run as he does, but he says to her, "You ought to do it; you should not be in bed; why are you always ill?" He forgets that she cannot help it. The fat cattle are not to push the lean cattle with horn and with shoulder, lest they trample the weak ones under their feet. No, the Lord would have Mr. Great-heart say to Mr. Feeble-mind, "We will wait for you, if you cannot walk so fast as we do; and"—notice that,—"we will deny ourselves even that which would be lawful for us for your sake; there are some things which would lead you into sin, we will not do them lest you should be injured; they might not hurt us, but we will not do them lest in any way you should be made to suffer."

All things are lawful to me, all the common actions of life are lawful for me, but there are times when they are not expedient.

"We will not enter into doubtful disputations before you," said the great but gracious leader. We will not tax you with sermons upon very high doctrines that would only trouble you. Questions that would not minister to your growth in grace shall be left for a while; we will discuss difficult subjects in your absence. We will say to one another, "We have a tough point to settle, but we will leave it till he is gone down to the prayer-meeting or when he is stopping at home because his head aches; we will not talk about such matters till all the weak saints are out of the way." If father and mother have anything that is nasty to say to one another, they must not let anyone else hear it. "Pray do not let the children know anything about it," they say to each other. Whenever you and I who are the strong members of the church, have certain thorny matters to consider, we must not do it before the new-born converts. Let us say, "We must get all the children away before we talk about these things;" and as we are sure, I hope, to have newborn souls always among us, we had better endeavour to keep clear of these doubtful disputations altogether.

The very sweet point in the story is where Mr. Ready-to-halt comes up on his crutches. Now, Mr. Ready-to-halt, and Mr. Feeble-mind, you will be at home; there are two of you. You poor weak saints, who need all the help you can get, it is quite right that you should come in, because there are some more just like you in the church, and you can help each other. How, delightful it was when Mr. Ready-to-halt said he would lend Mr. Feeble-mind one of his crutches. But I do like the way that Feeble-mind firmly declined the loan. If he was feeble-minded, he was not lame; and, therefore, he said, "I am not inclined to halt before I am lame." I suppose that this good man, Ready-to-halt, had been accustomed to use a form of prayer. Feeble-mind, on the other hand, could say, "My prayers are very poor, brother; still, they are my own words, and they are the expression of my inmost feelings." He did not blame Ready-to-halt for having crutches, but he would not use them himself. Some people say to me, "We wish you would write us a book of prayers, as you have given us two volumes of Readings and 'The Interpreter';" but I reply, "I cannot make prayers for you, I cannot conscientiously set up for a crutch-maker. Still, you had better go on crutches, and read a prayer in the family, than not pray at all." I like to hear

Mr. Feeble-mind, as he draws himself up, and says, as it were, "No, no, no, I have not come to need crutches yet, though they might be useful against a dog. They are of some use, perhaps, and you manage, somehow, to get along on them." Still, it shows the good heart there was in Ready-to-halt that he was willing to lend Mr. Feeble-mind one of his crutches. Many saints have crutches of one sort or another, they cannot trust their feet, and they have found them to be some help to them, and they are generally willing to lend their crutches to others. It is quite right that it should be so. Now, come in, friend Ready-to-halt, with your crutches; come in, Mr. Feeble-mind with all you weakness and fears, you two will then take counsel together about the things of God. We will wait for you, and will not mind what we do so long as we can get to the same end together by-and-by.

A little further on, we find that Ready-to-halt, after Giant Despair was killed, danced with one of his crutches in his hand in a very wonderful manner; and, just ere they passed over the river, poor Feeble-mind left his feeble mind to be buried by Mr. Valiant in a dunghill, and Mr. Ready-to-halt bequeathed his crutches to his son, for he did not need such things in Heaven.

One day, I was sitting under the olives at Mentone,

and saw a sheep that had evidently strayed away from the rest of the flock, and lost itself. It was bleating because it was all alone, and did not know its way back. Presently, a whistle was blown, and the sheep was off immediately in the direction from which the sound came. The Lord says, "My sheep hear My voice, and I know them, and they follow Me." They know His call even when He whistles to them; and I do believe, dear brethren, that you would sooner hear the Gospel whistle than you would hear the new doctrines preached in the best possible manner; for there is, somehow or other, a ring in the true Gospel which you cannot mistake. If it is real Gospel, you will know the voice of it, you will say, "That is my way, and I am off in response to the gracious call."

You should get to the Shepherd, and you should get among the sheep, and be not long a lone sheep. There are some brethren who will be glad to see you. The elders will be glad to see you. I am not lame, yet I would buy a pair of crutches to go with you if you cannot go by any other means; but I will lend you both of them, for I shall not require them myself. One is glad to be able to rejoice in the Lord, and go forward, running in the way of His salvation; but our joy is doubled if we can encourage Mr. Feeble-mind and Mr. Ready-to-halt.

MR. FEEBLE-MIND AND MR. READY-TO-HALT

"Rather than we will part, I will lend thee one of my crutches."

XX.

CHRISTIANA AT THE GATE AND THE RIVER.

WHEN Christiana, the wife of Christian, went on pilgrimage, she, of course, went through the same gate as her husband. Thus the story runs:—

"Wherefore, methought I saw Christiana and Mercy, and the boys, go all of them up to the gate; to which, when they were come, they betook themselves to a short debate about how they must manage their calling at the gate, and what should be said to Him that did open to them. So it was concluded, since Christiana was the eldest, that she should knock for entrance, and that she should speak to Him that did open, for the rest. So Christiana began to knock; and, as her poor husband did, she knocked, and knocked again. But, instead of any that answered, they all thought that they heard as if a dog came barking upon them; a dog, and a great one too, and this made the women and children afraid; nor durst they, for a while, to knock any more, for fear the mastiff should fly upon them. Now, therefore, they were greatly tumbled up and down in their minds, and knew not what to do: knock they durst not, for fear of the dog; go back they durst not, for fear the Keeper of that gate should espy them as they so went, and should be offended with them. At last, they thought of knocking again, and knocked more vehemently than they did at the first. Then said the Keeper of the gate, 'Who is there?' So the dog left off to bark, and He opened unto them."

When Bunyan is talking of a strong man's experiences, he represents arrows as being shot at him. When he speaks of women and children, he represents them as being barked at by a dog. Some timid souls are as alarmed at the baying of a dog as stouter hearts at the flight of flaming darts.

God does not allow the feeble to be tempted to the same extent as the strong. They are not shot at with fiery arrows; a savage dog barks at them instead. When I am describing the sore temptations of certain Christians, some of you say within yourselves, "But we have never felt anything like that." Now, do not be vexed with yourselves because you have not had so trying an experience, but be thankful for it. Rejoice that you got in, like Christiana and Mercy, with only a dog to bark at you. The arrows are not to be desired. If, when you came to the Lord Jesus Christ, all the opposition that you met with was nothing more than the mere barking of a dog that could not even bite you, be grateful that you came so easily, and that Satan was held in check so that he was unable to molest you.

Everything, in all the world, that would keep a sinner from coming to Christ, is nothing better than a dog's bark. There is not much cause for alarm in the barking of a dog at a distance. If, when I was coming to this Tabernacle, I heard a dog barking, I do not know that I should take much notice of it. If I were in my house at night, and heard a barking dog, it might disturb my sleep, but it would not alarm me very much. If a man were going upon some important mission, and some little whipper-snapper of a cur came yelping at his heels, he would not trouble to notice it. All that devils, or men, can ever say against a soul that comes to Christ, and trusts in Him, is not a whit more to be feared than a dog's bark. Therefore, I pray you, vex not your heart because of it. Say in your soul, "Christ bids me come, and I will not be kept back by a dog's bark. Christ calls me; I hear God's voice; I accept Heaven's invitation; let the dogs bark till they are weary, if they will; such sweet music is sounding in my ear as drowns their howlings.

> "'I'll go to Jesus, though my sin
>   Hath like a mountain rose;
> I know His courts, I'll enter in,
>   Whatever may oppose.'"

I ask you now to listen to what happened when the pilgrims got inside. They all entered save Mercy, and she was left without, trembling and crying, as some do after their companions have found peace.

However, Mercy knocked again; and, after a while, the Keeper of the gate opened it, and she was admitted, and all were welcome and forgiven by the Lord of the way.

"So He left them a while, in a summer parlour below, where they entered into talk by themselves; and thus Christiana began: 'O Lord, how glad am I that we are got in hither!'

"Mercy. So you well may; but I of all have cause to leap for joy.

"Chris. I thought one time, as I stood at the gate (because I had knocked, and none did answer)), that all our labour had been lost, especially when that ugly cur made such a heavy barking against us.

"Mercy. But my worst fear was after I saw that you were taken into His favour, and that I was left behind Now, thought I, it is fulfilled which is written, 'Two women shall be grinding together; the one shall be taken, and the other left.' (Matt. xxiv. 41.) I had much ado to forbear crying out, 'Undone! Undone!' And afraid I was to knock any more; but when I looked up to what was written over the gate, I took courage. I also thought that I must either knock again, or die; so I knocked, but I cannot tell how, for my spirit now struggled betwixt life and death.

"Chris. Can you not tell how you knocked? I am sure your knocks were so earnest, that the very sound of them made me start; I thought I never heard such knocking in all my life; I thought you would have come in by violent hands, or have taken the Kingdom by storm. (Matt. xi. 12.)

"Mercy. Alas! to be in my case, who that so was could but have done so? You saw that the door was shut upon me, and that there was a most cruel dog thereabout. Who, I say, that was so faint-hearted as I, that would not have knocked with all their might? But, pray, what said my Lord to my rudeness? Was He not angry with me?

"CHRIS. When He heard your lumbering noise, He gave a wonderful innocent smile; I believe what you did pleased Him well enough, for He showed no sign to the contrary. But I marvel in my heart why He keeps such a dog; had I known that before, I fear I should not have had heart enough to have ventured myself in this manner. But now we are in, we are in; and I am glad with all my heart.

"MERCY. I will ask, if you please, next time He comes down, why He keeps such a filthy cur in His yard. I hope He will not take it amiss.

"'Ay, do,' said the children, 'and persuade Him to hang him; for we are afraid he will bite us when we go hence.'"

You see the children wanted the dog hanged, like the negro who said, "If God is so much stronger than de debil, why doesn't he kill de debil?" I have often wished the same, but it does not so please the Master.

"So at last He came down to them again, and Mercy fell to the ground on her face before Him, and worshipped, and said, 'Let my Lord accept of the sacrifice of praise which I now offer unto Him with the calves of my lips.'

"So He said unto her, 'Peace be to thee: stand up.' But she continued upon her face, and said, 'Righteous art Thou, O Lord, when I plead with Thee; yet let me talk with Thee of Thy judgments.' (Jeremiah xii. 1.) 'Wherefore dost Thou keep so cruel a dog in Thy yard, at the sight of which, such women and children as we, are ready to fly from Thy gate for fear?'

"He answered and said, 'That dog has another owner, he also is kept close in another man's ground, only My pilgrims hear his barking; he belongs to the castle which you see there at a distance, but can come up to the walls of this place. He has frighted many an honest pilgrim from worse to better, by the great voice of his roaring. Indeed, he that owneth him doth not keep him out of any goodwill to Me or Mine, but with intent to keep the pilgrims from coming to Me, and that they may be afraid to knock at this gate for entrance. Sometimes also he has broken out, and has worried some that I loved; but I take all at present patiently. I also give My pilgrims timely help, so they are not delivered to his power, to do to them what his doggish nature would prompt him to. But what! my purchased one, I trow, hadst thou known never so much beforehand, thou wouldst not have been afraid of a dog. The beggars that go from door to door will, rather than they will lose a supposed alms, run the hazard of the bawling, barking, and biting, too, of a dog; and shall a dog—a dog in another man's yard, a dog whose barking I turn to the profit of pilgrims,—keep any from coming to Me? I deliver them from the lions, my darling from the power of the dog.' "

So, the temptations of poor seeking souls do not come from the Holy Spirit. They come from the devil. Note that the Lord said, "I take all at present patiently." God shows His great longsuffering, I think, in bearing even with the devil himself. Moreover, He added that He turned the barking of the dog to the profit of the pilgrims. Some of them would come up to the gate half asleep; but when the dog

barked, it caused them to be in earnest. It has been
well said that a roaring devil is to be preferred to a
sleeping devil. It is better to be full of fear and
trembling than it is to be asleep. So the Lord over-
rules the temptations of Satan for the good of poor
coming sinners. Well then, do not hang the dog, but
let him be turned to good account. Only, poor sinner,
fear him not. Come to Jesus, trembler. May the
Holy Spirit enable thee to come, and take him to be
thine for ever and ever, and then let the dogs bark as
loudly as they please.

*   *   *   *   , *

Now let us pass to the end of the wonderful dream,
and see Christiana and her friends at the river's brink.

How, think you, did the pilgrims, who dwelt in the
Land of Beulah, regard death? It was by no means a
subject for sorrow. Here is the charming description
of the joys of Heaven's borderland :—

"After this, I beheld until they were come unto the Land
of Beulah, where the sun shineth night and day. Here,
because they are weary, they betook themselves a while to
rest; and, because this country was common for pilgrims,
and because the orchard and vineyards that were here
belonged to the King of the Celestial country, therefore they
were licensed to make bold with any of His things. But a
little while soon refreshed them here; for the bells did so
ring, and the trumpets continually sound so melodiously,
that they could not sleep; and yet they received as much

refreshing as if they had slept their sleep ever so soundly.
Here also the noise of them that walked in the streets, was,
'More pilgrims are come to town.'   And another would
answer, saying, 'And so many went over the water, and
were let in at the golden gates to-day.'   They would cry
again, 'There is now a legion of Shining Ones just come
to town, by which we know that there are more pilgrims
upon the road; for here they come to wait for them, and to
comfort them after all their sorrow.'   Then the Pilgrims
got up and walked to and fro; but how were their ears now
filled with heavenly noises, and their eyes delighted with
celestial visions!   In this land they heard nothing, saw
nothing, felt nothing, smelt nothing, tasted nothing, that
was offensive to their stomach or mind; only when they
tasted of the water of the river over which they were to go,
they thought that tasted a little bitterish to the palate, but it
proved sweet when it was down."

Their great joy was that other pilgrims were arriving where they were, and that some were crossing
the river every day.   The saints who have reached
Beulah Land ought to be rejoicing as they hear of
pilgrims crossing the river.   If we have full faith, we
shall think with great joy of the dear ones who have
gone in to see the King in His beauty; and, instead of
saying mournfully, "They are dead," we shall exclaim
triumphantly, "They are now beyond the reach of
death!"   Instead of supposing that we have lost them,
we shall realize that they have only preceded us a
little while; we are on the road, and shall soon reach

home, and blessed shall be the day when we rejoin them in glory.

"Now while they lay here, and waited for the good hour, there was a noise in the town, that there was a post come from the Celestial City, with matter of great importance to one Christiana, the wife of Christian the Pilgrim. So inquiry was made for her, and the house was found where she was; so the post presented her with a letter; the contents whereof were, 'Hail, good woman! I bring thee tidings that the Master calleth for thee, and expecteth that thou shouldest stand in His presence, in clothes of immortality, within these ten days.'

"When he had read this letter to her, he gave her therewith a sure token that he was a true messenger, and was come to bid her make haste to be gone. The token was, an arrow with a point sharpened with love, let easily into her heart, which by degrees wrought so effectually with her, that at the time appointed she must be gone."

Well, so it is with pilgrims still; they have their arrows sharpened with love, a month, or a year, or more before the time appointed for them to be gone. They receive notice that the Master expects them soon; and they ripen, and mellow in spirit.

"When Christiana saw that her time was come, and that she was the first of this company that was to go over, she called for Mr. Great-heart, her guide, and told him how matters were. So he told her he was heartily glad of the news, and could have been glad had the post come for him. Then she bid that he should give advice how all things should be prepared for her journey. So he told her, saying,

'Thus and thus it must be; and we that survive will accompany you to the river side.'

"Then she called for her children, and gave them her blessing and told them, that she yet read with comfort the mark that was set in their foreheads, and was glad to see them with her there, and that they had kept their garments so white. Lastly, she bequeathed to the poor that little she had, and commanded her sons and her daughters to be ready against the messenger should come for them."

As soon as Christiana received her token, she did what most Christian people do, she sent for her minister, whose name was Mr. Great-heart, for he had helped her and her family on pilgrimage till they had come to the river; and what, think you, did Mr. Great-heart say, when she told him that an arrow had entered into her heart? Did he sit down and cry with her? No, "he told her he was heartily glad of the news, and could have been glad had the post come for him." And, though I am not Mr. Great-heart, I can truly say the same. You and I should not dread this message, but may even long for it, envying those who precede us into the presence of the Well-beloved, and get the first chance of leaning their heads upon that bosom whence they shall never wish to lift them again, for therein they find joy and bliss for ever.

Christiana did not look upon her departure with any regret; she took loving adieux of her children and all her friends and fellow-pilgrims. Neither do our dear friends, who are summond from our side, look forward to death with any kind of apprehension. When we sit and talk with them about the world to come, our conversation is that of those who would rejoice when any one of us entered into rest, and would be confident of meeting again on the other side of the river.

"Now the day drew on, that Christiana must be gone. So the road was full of people to see her take her journey. But, behold, all the banks beyond the river were full of horses and chariots, which were come down from above to accompany her to the city gate. So she came forth, and entered the river, with a beckon of farewell to those that followed her to the river side. The last words that she was heard to say here, were, 'I come, Lord, to be with Thee, and bless Thee.'

"So her children and friends returned to their place, for those that waited for Christiana had carried her out of their sight. So she went and called, and entered in at the gate with all the ceremonies of joy that her husband Christian had done before her. At her departure her children wept. But Mr. Great-heart and Mr. Valiant played upon the well-tuned cymbal and harp for joy."

What do you think they say in Heaven about our dear ones who fall asleep in Jesus? Why, the angels shall come to meet them! Lazarus died, and was carried by angels into Abraham's bosom, and that is what happens to all the saints. Yes, the angels come to meet the saints, and to escort them to their eternal seats. They do not mourn when the sons of God come to glory. They stretch out their glittering hands, and say, "Welcome, brother; welcome, sister! You have long been pilgrims; now you shall rest for ever. Welcome to your eternal home!"

And how do you suppose the saints in light regard the arrival of those who come a little later? Doubtless, they welcome them with gladsome acclamations; and all through the golden streets they run crying, "More pilgrims are come to town! More pilgrims are come to town! More redeemed ones have come home!" And the Lord Jesus Christ smiles, and says, "Father, I thank Thee because those whom Thou hast given Me are with Me where I am." He welcomes them. And God the Father, too, is glad to greet them in glory. Are you not all glad when your children come home? Lives there a man among you who does not rejoice to see his boys and girls come back to him even for the brief holidays? We like to hear their sweet voices, though they do trouble us sometimes; but then they are our own children, our own offspring, and somehow, to our ears, there is no voice so sweet as theirs; and to God there is no music like the voices of His children. He is glad to get them home to Himself, to go no more out for ever. And the blessed

Spirit, too, let us not forget Him,—He delights to see the holy souls He formed anew, those with whom He strove, with whom He wrought so many years. As a workman rejoices over his perfected workmanship, so does the Spirit of God rejoice over those whom He has made to be partakers of the inheritance of the saints in light.

Bunyan puts it beautifully,—

"But glorious it was to see how the upper region was filled with horses and chariots, with trumpeters and pipers, with singers and players on stringed instruments, to welcome the Pilgrims as they went up, and followed one another in at the beautiful gate of the city."

Brothers and sisters, if you are in Christ, do not be afraid to die, for dying grace shall be given to you for your dying moments.

Remember how these pilgrims crossed the river. Mr. Stand-fast said, "The waters, indeed, are to the palate bitter, and to the stomach cold; yet the thoughts of what I am going to, and of the convoy that waits for me on the other side, lie as a glowing coal at my heart." He also said, "This river has been a terror to many; yea, the thoughts of it have also often frightened me. Now, methinks, I stand easy, my foot is fixed upon that on which the feet of the priests that bare the ark of the covenant stood, while Israel went over this Jordan."

Remember how poor Mr. Ready-to-halt left his crutches behind him. Are you not glad of that, dear friend, you who have been ready-to-halt for years? There was dear old Mr. Feeble-mind, who said to Valiant-for-truth, "As for my feeble mind, that I will leave behind me, for that I have no need of it in the place whither I go. Nor is it worth bestowing upon the poorest pilgrim; wherefore, when I am gone, I desire that you, Mr. Valiant, would bury it in a dung-hill." And then there was poor Mr. Despondency, with his daughter Much-afraid, who crossed the stream together. "The last words of Mr. Despondency were, 'Farewell night, welcome day.'" As for Miss Much-afraid, she went through the river singing, but no-body could make out quite what the words were, she seemed to be beyond the power of expressing her de-light.

Oh, it is wonderful how these pilgrims do when they come to die! They may tremble while they live; but they do not tremble when they die. The weakest of them become the strongest then. I have helped many pilgrims on the way, and among them some Mr. Feeble-minds and Mr. Fearings, and a very great worry have they been to me while on the road; but, at the last, either the river has been empty, and they have gone over dry-shod, or else, when they have come to the very depths of it, they have played the man so well, that I have been astounded. I never imagined that they could have been so brave. They have stumbled at a straw before; but in death they have climbed mountains. They have been the most weak, timid, sparrow-like people that you could meet with; and now they take to themselves eagle's wings wherewith to fly away.

Wherefore I counsel you, go to the graves of your loved ones with songs of gladness. Stand there, and if you drop a tear let the smile of your gratitude to God light it up, and transform it into a gem; and then go home, each one of you, and wait trustfully until your own change comes. As for myself, as I have often reminded you at the close of our joyous Sabbath services in the great congregation at the Tabernacle, so would I say again,—

"All that remains for me
Is but to love and sing,
And wait until the angels come
To bear me to their King."

CHRISTIANA AND HER CHILDREN

"She said to her children, 'Sons, we are all undone.' "

SETS BY
CHARLES HADDON SPURGEON
(1834 - 1892)

Pilgrim Publications is the only source for exact reprints of sets by C.H. Spurgeon which were originally published by Spurgeon's London publisher, Passmore & Alabaster, in the last century. All books are unedited and unabridged.

- **THE NEW PARK STREET PULPIT** consists of the first six volumes of the Spurgeon sermon series, covering the years 1855-1860, sermons #1-347. Our edition is in three large double-volumes, two years to each book.

- **THE METROPOLITAN TABERNACLE PULPIT** consists of volume 7 thru volume 63 of the Spurgeon sermon series, covering years 1861 thru 1917, sermons #348-3561.

- **THE TREASURY OF DAVID** is the seven-volume commentary on the Book of Psalms, twenty years in the making and the most extensive work ever accomplished on this book.

- **THE SWORD AND THE TROWEL** is a series of volumes containing the miscellaneous writings of Spurgeon as published in his monthly magazine, beginning in 1865. Sermons, tracts, editorials, book reviews, conference addresses, outlines, letters, and other materials are reprinted unedited.

- **LECTURES TO MY STUDENTS** consists of the original four volumes in this series and for the first time reprinted unabridged in one durable clothbound edition.

Ask for these books at your local Christian book store. Consult a current price list (free on request) for current prices.

Pilgrim PUBLICATIONS P.O. Box 66, Pasadena, Texas 77501

Metropolitan Tabernacle Pulpit
❖
The New Park Street Pulpit
❖

Spurgeon's sermons were preached at New Park Street Chapel (1855-1860) and the Metropolitan Tabernacle (1861-1892). They were recorded by stenographers and published yearly, as follows:

NEW PARK STREET PULPIT: Volumes 1-6, Years 1855-1860

METROPOLITAN TABERNACLE PULPIT:
Volumes 7-63, Years 1861-1917

The entire series consists of 3,561 numbered sermons. This is a publishing record for number of sermons, consecutive weekly issues, consecutive yearly volumes, and number of volumes in a sermon series.

Wilbur M. Smith called it "the greatest sermon set in the English language." **B. H. Carroll** said the sermons "constitute a complete body of systematic theology." **Dr. W. A. Criswell** says, "Never have I read anywhere or in any literature anything that compares to the sermons of C. H. Spurgeon."

The Pilgrim reprint edition of Spurgeon's sermons is **complete, unedited,** and **unabridged.** All other sets or selections of Spurgeon's sermons are excerpted from the 3,561 we are publishing.

See your local book dealer about this set; if there is no dealer in your area, write to the publisher for a price list for this set and other Spurgeon books which we publish.

AT YOUR LOCAL BOOK STORE

Original Titles by C. H. Spurgeon (1834 - 1892)
Published by Pilgrim PUBLICATIONS, Pasadena, Texas